MARTIAN TIME

James Hart

Cover by Brittney Nunes

Edited by James Hart

Acknowledgements

Thanks to Brittney Nunes for all her work on the cover and inspiring me to keep writing. She has also encouraged some young writers, Allie Kat (not her real name, check with her parents) and Taylor King, and I encourage you to check out the stories of all of them as well.

In the short story prequel, **The Fourth Patient**, a man who is an average Joe does something extraordinary when he thought he was just going to a doctor's appointment and gets pulled into a wormhole in the center of San Francisco. Will he be trapped somewhere else in space and time? Once we know the man, we are now ready for the mission, fifteen years later, in **Martian Time**, where as head of Mission Control he leads the first manned mission to Mars, including Dave Whitney, his wife Kate, and their teenage daughters Kristy and Brandy. But when the crew vanishes on their descent to Mars, does the evidence point to a connection to what happened to Joe in San Francisco?

The Fourth Patient

(a Martian Time prequel)

by James Hart

Chapter One

It was a rainy day in San Francisco, and not one of those 'run between the drops' rains. This one was a drencher. It was a good thing Joe Schmoe remembered to bring his umbrella from his home as he had to walk from his workplace after work to the doctor's office for an appointment before then walking to the BART station to head home to the East Bay for the night. It was another long day, and he was mentally and physically exhausted as usual. He had done the work commute routine for several years now. He was not a young man anymore, and it seemed this was the year when his gray hairs began to outnumber all the rest of his hair. Joe was exactly six feet tall. He had always been six feet tall. So, he couldn't understand what was wrong with the height measurement on that doctor's scale last time that said he was five feet eleven inches tall. His driver's license told him he was six feet tall. Nothing could ever change that.

Nonetheless, he moved as quickly as he could through the rain and approached the office of Benjamin Gonzalez, M.D. Yes, a doctor with a

Mexican name in a Japanese neighborhood, who didn't speak a word of Spanish or Japanese, and didn't even have a discernible accent. Joe had a 4:00 p.m. appointment but arrived in the waiting room at 4:02 p.m., which is well within the buffer of error. Of course, in Joe's line of work, a two-minute error could mean missing a successful planetary landing, but that's another story, and it would never happen on his watch. Being two minutes late to the doctor is so commonplace that he should be welcomed in immediately with no questions asked. Besides, when was the last time that Joe was late or missed any appointment? Exactly! Joe was organized. He had all his days planned out on his calendar at least a month in advance. And he made sure to set reminders for himself, so he never missed an appointment. If you looked in the dictionary under dependable, there was a picture of Joe. Had it not been for the rain and the pedestrians in his way, always stopping unpredictably to window shop, he would have arrived exactly at 4:00. Yet, despite his reasonable arrival time, he still had quite a wait and he was not happy about it and he was ready to make his displeasure felt at the very first opportunity. This would certainly impact evening activities on his calendar.

"Mr. Schmoe, the doctor will see you now," the receptionist muttered, as if everything were fine and it was no big deal.

"Well, it's about time!", said Joe in frustration. "I've been waiting for 45 minutes. I have places to go and things to do." *Fall asleep on the couch with his hand in a bag of barbecued potato chips with the TV on.*

"Sorry. The doctor was double-booked today. You were his second 4:00."

"Well, that doesn't make any sense. He can't see two patients at the same time. He's an educated man. He should realize that."

"Actually, he *can* and actually often sees *three* patients at the same time. He is quite proficient at going back and forth between rooms. That's why there are five patient rooms and only one doctor. Besides that, you would be surprised at how many people cancel, even without notice, and the doctor's time *is* valuable."

"I know. I can tell by his prices. But so is my time. I may change the world one day, but not if I'm stuck here."

"Well, you could choose a different doctor, but to get the best sometimes requires that you wait."

"Does he pay you to say that?"

"He will see you in room three."

Yes, she totally ignored that last question. It occurred to Joe that perhaps the doctor was not so much different from him, filling up his time as much as possible so no precious second is wasted. As Joe walked down the long hallway to room three, he had to go past rooms four and five. He heard someone knocking on the inside of room five and trying to open the door. *I wonder how long he's been waiting.* Joe always used the restroom before going into the doctor so that he would not be put in the predicament of being stuck in a room holding it with nowhere to go. He imagined this patient probably forgot to go before he came. He probably thought the doctor would have him pee in a cup and he wanted to have some ready, just in case, but doctors hardly ask you to do that anymore.

It was an older office in an older neighborhood and the numbers on the doors of the rooms were faded or missing and so apparently, they expected you to count the doors to find the right one, but being familiar with the office, Joe found his way to room three. He walked into this room, and of course, he somehow arrived before the doctor, who no doubt was probably still with another patient. He evaluated his situation to determine how to best use the time before the doctor's arrival, to 'beat the system', in other words. *I'm accustomed to outsmarting others to make the best of my time, but this doctor is clever.*

There was a single uncomfortable chair to sit on, or option two was the exam table with that noisy paper they use to protect you from the germs of the last person that was in here. It was already rolled out on the table, so Joe had to be sure it was a fresh piece and not just left from the last patient. So would Joe choose to sit in the uncomfortable chair, or would he sit on the table that the doctor would probably tell him to sit on when he came in anyway? Should he strip down to his underwear now to move things along? *If I wait, he is going to say when he walks in, "Strip down to your underwear." Then he's going to leave for ten minutes to see somebody in another room even though it only takes me a minute to undress. He'll use that as an excuse.* Joe wasn't falling for that. If he were to undress now, then the doctor wouldn't be able to blame him for his own delay. He would have to stay and see Joe right away. Just as Joe had stripped down to his underwear and seated himself on the crunchy paper on the exam table, his doctor's nurse walked in without knocking.

"Excuse me," she said. "I need cotton balls. This is the only room with cotton balls." She pulled some from a drawer and walked back out, leaving the door wide open, and with it, a cold chill. A couple of other patients walked by and looked in while passing. Joe got up from the table to shut the door.

After another 15 minutes, the doctor entered. "How are we doing today?"

"First of all, there is only one of me, and he's exhausted from overwork and lack of sleep. And I've been waiting in your office far too long. My appointment was for 4:00, and now it's after 5:00."

"I recommend morning appointments. The day always starts on time. Too many things can go wrong by 4:00."

"I'm on the road by 6:00 a.m. to get to work by 8:00 a.m. and I can't get off work in the morning. That would totally disrupt my day."

"What if you're sick? Then you're forced to be off. And I assure you the world will keep going even if you miss a day."

"I'm never sick, I mean, not sick enough to miss work. Real men don't take sick days."

"That's not a good philosophy. Some of those 'real men' die at age 50 and it could have been prevented. Looking at your medical record, I see you're getting close to the big 5-0. What do you do for work that's so important that they can't live without you?"

"If I told you, I'd probably have to kill you."

"I doubt it's that secretive. I could just find it in your insurance records."

"Okay, you got me. I'm a scientist studying ways to speed up space travel. We want to make interstellar travel possible. It's the next space race, and we have to get the upper hand. That's about as much as I'm allowed to say, in case you might be a Russian spy."

"With a name like Gonzalez? I don't think so."

"But that's all part of your cover. If you had a long name that nobody could pronounce that started with a V, it would be too obvious."

"Is that the way you live your life, suspicious of everyone being a spy?"

"It's worked for me so far. I've been doing this for over 20 years."

"You won't make many friends that way."

"That's okay. I don't need a lot of friends."

"People usually only say that until they find out that they do need those friends after learning the hard way. No man is an island. Friends are a valuable resource. I suggest you find some. So, you study stuff like warp drives, wormholes and the like? Earth not good enough for you?"

"One day we'll need another place to live. We have to start planning sometime."

"Is that a fact?", said the doctor with a doubtful tone. "That's not really top on my to do list. All the stuff I enjoy is right here on earth. And if we take care of this one we should do just fine. Do you really think you're going to find an earth as good as ours?"

"It has to be out there. We can start with Mars, at least to gain vital experience. If we put our minds to it, we can make any place work for us if it's good real estate, in the habitable zone."

"Well Mars might be lacking a few of the comforts of life I enjoy, like food and air. It's not in my habitable zone. But I'm sure people are lining up to go, because people are into that sort of thing. So you're in here today for your checkup, but *also* because you're concerned about your heart?"

"I've been having some chest pains I'm concerned about."

"Any history of heart problems in your family?"

"Not that I am aware of. I don't exactly keep track of my family history. I'm focused on my work."

"Those symptoms are common. I'm not *that* concerned."

"That's because it's not *your* heart."

    "We can do an EKG just to check it out, but it may just be stress. Could be that secretive job of yours. You need to learn to relax. Try not to carry the weight of the world on your shoulders. Trust me, the world isn't really keeping track. And stop distrusting people like they're spies and treat them like people."

    "I'll have more time to relax once I figure out how to get people to Mars in 30 days or less. We're studying a new propulsion system."

    "The problem is, once you think you're set to relax, you move straight to your next issue, and you're always one step away from reaching your goal. You just need to give yourself some Joe time."

    "Honestly, I probably won't do that unless I'm forced to do so."

    "Then maybe you should go to Mars to get away. Do you speak Martian or any other languages?"

    "Martian isn't a language, yet, but I do speak some Japanese."

    "And how is that working out for you?"

    "Since I work in Japantown here in the City, it comes in handy."

"And what about dealing with radiation?"

"I wear SPF 50."

"No, I mean in space travel. All that radiation is going to affect people. You're talking about long-term time in space. Don't you have a doctor on your staff to tell you these things?"

"We're working on materials that provide more protection against radiation."

"Doctor's work with radiation all the time, so if you find some practical uses for that on earth, you be sure to let me know. In fact, if you have enough to provide protection for at least one person, bring it in and we'll test it out the next time you need an X-ray."

"I can bring a rather large piece. It's a relatively thin, fabric like substance that rolls out and unfolds and could even cover a group of people. It could provide protection from high levels of radiation on an alien planet."

"Or here on earth."

"Yes, I suppose here on earth as well."

"Okay, tell you what… I'll get a blood sample from you that will tell me what I need to know, and we can get you in here tomorrow and do some more tests if needed and make sure everything is okay. And I'll let you know what the blood tests reveal. But if I can't figure it out I'll tell you it's all in your head and prescribe placebo for you. That works on at least ten percent of my patients, as long as I don't tell them. Just talk to my receptionist to schedule the appointment, after you get your clothes back on. And next time don't undress unless I tell you to do so. It wasn't necessary, and now you have to waste that valuable time of yours getting dressed again. Life is too short for that, sometimes shorter than we think."

Joe responded in frustration, "Sure thing doc. Just don't leave me waiting out there."

"Well, we don't call it a waiting room for nothing. I wish I didn't need it and could make it into my break room. Of course, I'm like you and don't take breaks. But I promise I'll get you in right away tomorrow. Our national security and earth's future depend upon it."

"Are you being sarcastic? Never mind. See you tomorrow." Joe walked back out to the waiting room and talked with the receptionist. "So, the doctor says to schedule me for tomorrow."

"*Really? That soon?* Let me check because I'm pretty sure we're all booked solid." She did her usual typing and mouse clicking while looking at the computer screen. She had a serious look on her face like this was going to be a problem. "We have a lot of patients tomorrow.

He is showing he can fit you in at 3:30, even though he already has three others scheduled for 3:30. You would be the fourth patient at that time. Look! Let me just put you in for two weeks from today, and you will be the first patient at the scheduled time. He will not even remember that he told you to come in tomorrow. He's always telling people to come back tomorrow, but he never looks at his schedule. That makes my job more difficult. Plus, he missed a day last week and is still trying to catch up for that."

"But he promised to get me right in, and I can't really wait two weeks. I'll just come and take my chances. I just want to get this over with."

The receptionist glanced around the waiting room in all directions before signaling Joe to come closer and lean toward her. Then, speaking just above a whisper while looking intently at him, she said: *"You don't understand. You don't want to be the fourth patient."*

"I know I don't, but I really need to come. I've got to fit these things in where I can."

"No, you don't understand. He rarely schedules four patients at one time. I've only seen it a few times, and each time…"

The doctor peeked his head into the room and asked the receptionist, "Sharon, is everything okay?"

"Oh, yes, doctor," she quickly replied, feeling embarrassed at being caught off guard like that. "Everything is fine."

"So, Joe, we'll see you tomorrow," said the doctor. "Be sure to get a good night's rest, and I'd love to see that new invention of yours."

"Okay, doc. I'll do it for you." Just as Joe was leaving, he scanned the waiting room and noticed a sickly child sitting there alone. "Hello there. Are your parents here? Is everything okay?" Joe actually surprised himself because he rarely pays attention to things like that. The child just gave him a blank stare. "Do you understand me?" Since the child was Japanese, Joe tried asking him in Japanese if he was okay. "Daijōbudesuka?" He looked back at Joe with half a smile and then looked the other way, clearly lethargic. The receptionist then called to the child and he got up to go see the doctor. On that note Joe saw time getting away from him and was ready for his walk to his train with umbrella in hand so that he could get home in time to go to sleep and come back to work tomorrow.

Chapter Two

Joe got off at the Dublin BART station and walked to his car in the parking lot. He couldn't stop thinking about what the receptionist was trying to tell him. The doctor was hiding something. But why? *Should I cancel the appointment? Should I just not show up?* Just then he started feeling those chest pains again, as if to remind him that he needed to return to the doctor. Maybe it was just indigestion. Maybe he was just worrying too much. Maybe the doctor was right. Stress was just making him sick. He just needed to stop worrying and relax. It wasn't like that doctor was part of some huge conspiracy theory or something. And he was certainly no spy trying to discover secrets from Joe. That would be ridiculous. He was just a good man trying to help a man like Joe, a graying, shrinking workaholic without a real life. *He would have no reason to try to deceive me… no, of course not.*

Joe started up his car and drove out of the lot. It was still another half hour drive to his home, if there were no traffic delays. As he got moving on the highway, a car immediately cut in front of him. He honked his horn in frustration. "You could have killed us, idiot!" Joe knew the driver couldn't hear him. He was long gone. But that was the life Joe was accustomed to, everyone always being in such a hurry, just thinking about themselves. Sometimes it seemed things were just spiraling out of control. Would he be better off going on some space mission and getting away from this rat race? What did he really have here? He experienced a failed marriage because he was married to his job. And where had this job gotten him? What purpose has it really served? He was still deep in debt, and he might never see the rewards of his hard work. Someone else will use the knowledge he had acquired after he was long gone. They would get the credit for achieving his goals. And now… another traffic jam. *Maybe I won't get a good night's sleep after all.*

The Next Day (for those of you who are keeping track)

Joe entered the waiting room ten minutes before his appointment time. He kept thinking about what the receptionist had told him yesterday. However, there was a different, younger woman there today in her place. "Hello, is Sharon here today?" he asked.

"Sharon?"

"Yes, the receptionist who is usually here. I spoke to her yesterday."

"I'm sorry," she responded. "This is my first day here."

"Oh, I see," said Joe. "Okay, I know I'm the fourth patient, but at least I'm a little early. I hope that helps."

"Oh, you're the fourth patient?", responded the receptionist, as if she were especially expecting him. "Go right into room five and wait for the doctor."

"Oh? Just like that? Okay, that's what I'm talking about!"

"Wait, wait, what's *that* you're carrying? You can't bring that in here."

"This is a material that protects against radiation. I told the doctor about it and he encouraged me to bring some. Imagine if you were on the moon exposed to solar radiation, but if you had this you could cover yourself in it and be protected from the radiation."

"But will it keep your blood from boiling in the 200 degree plus heat?"

"It provides a measure of protection from the heat, but you'll have a spacesuit for that."

"So it still needs work, and I bet it doesn't come with WiFi," she said. "Okay, I guess you can show it to the doctor. Is there anything I can get you before you go into the room?"

"No, I just want to see the doctor. I'm not sure... what do you mean by that?"

"Sorry, I was just thinking…", she said when she realized she had said too much. "Go on in."

Joe walked in beyond the receptionist desk and approached room five. He paused in his tracks. *Was she like asking for my last request? Is this some kind of cruel joke and everyone knows the punchline except for me?* For a second, he thought about just walking out of the office and never coming back. He dismissed the idea, not wanting to miss out on the benefits of arriving early, and so walked into the room, closing the door behind him, but still ready to run for it at the first sign of trouble. He opened the door again just to confirm that he could open it, and peaked out into the hallway.

The nurse who walked in on him in his underwear yesterday walked by rapidly without slowing down and said in one breath, "The doctor will be with you shortly," and yet, her tone seemed to suggest that she didn't even believe it, like that was what she was expected to say and told everyone without thinking about it.

"I am early for the appointment," he said, "but the doctor promised." She was already out of hearing range before he finished that sentence. Joe recalled that this was the same room someone was trying to get out of yesterday. *How could anyone have gotten locked in?* The door opened easily and everything appeared to be normal. Joe shut the door once again.

This was a nicer room than room three. It wasn't as stuffy as room three, which really did smell like cotton balls, (or was it mothballs?) and this room had a brighter look, even though there were no windows. It must have been the color scheme. It was a bit roomier, or at least seemed so, for some reason, probably because of the brighter colors. *In any case, they did get me in on time today. Finally I'm being respected.* As he looked around there was the usual exam table with paper laid on top of it, a sink, a computer station, and a stack of magazines. Doctors' offices had to provide enough reading material to keep patients from getting restless and make the time pass while they waited, perhaps nervously, for the doctor. Unfortunately, the quality of the reading material provided usually left much to be desired. Joe had no interest in reading the gossip magazine from two years ago.

He picked up a scientific magazine to page through while waiting to get this over with. Half of the pages were advertisements. He scanned through an article on autonomous vehicles. Then there was another article on all the uses for unmanned aerial vehicles. He thought about the unmanned vehicles that had been sent into space, and what his own work would accomplish. Joe noticed that one page was tabbed and that a small envelope was also holding that place in the magazine. *What could be so special about this page?* He noticed that there was some writing on the outside of the envelope. 'Do not open until 3:30'. *That's odd. Did someone write this today? There's no date, just a time. And 3:30 rolls around on a regular basis, like twice a day. Surely this isn't meant for me.* Curiously he checked his cell phone to find that the time was exactly 3:30. This seemed rather coincidental. He hesitated for a minute, but then listened quietly and didn't hear anyone coming, including that snoopy nurse, so he decided to quietly and quickly open the envelope to see what was inside. He found a letter-size piece of paper folded up with writing on the inside and so he unfolded it and read it to himself.

"Hello Joe. I apologize for the way I am presenting this. I believe you are a good man and will do the right thing. If you were looking for your life to have meaning, I may be able to help you out with that. I had a strange experience last week that I'm still trying to wrap my head around. I don't understand all of this quantum leap stuff or black holes or wormholes or whatever you call them. I'm just a doctor. A really good doctor for sure. Probably the best doctor *you'll* ever meet. But still, just a doctor. I visited a place last week and made it back, but I can't say the same for my brother. I may never see him again. And then there's the children. You saw one in the waiting room yesterday. He made it out. But there are more. A lot more. And there is so little time to save them. You are the last hope for the children. The other patients will be there waiting for you and together you can get the children out. When I heard what you did for a living and that you even spoke Japanese, I knew you had to be the one and that this had to be the day. Based on my calculations, you are in room five at the right time. If you brought that material to protect against radiation, you will probably need it to buy you the time you need. I wish I had better news, but I'm sorry to report that your tests reveal you have advanced heart disease and that you have already had one heart attack while apparently not being aware of it. You are suffering irreversible consequences from the abuse you brought upon yourself. Your dedication to your work to the neglect of your health was your downfall. I'm afraid I won't be seeing you again. Please make it count."

"What in the world?" Joe shouted as he jumped up and raced to open the door. *It's locked!* He began banging on the door. "Hello! Is anyone there? Please open the door!" He couldn't hear anyone coming. *Am I being ignored? Surely someone can hear me!* He pounded on the door again in vain, and then began to look for another way out. There was a closet, but that led nowhere. Could he break down the door? Apparently not, according to the health report he just got, and the insurance probably wouldn't cover the damage. Nevertheless, he tried kicking and pounding at it as hard as he could, with no effect. What about climbing out through the ceiling? He grabbed a chair and stood on it and attempted to reach the ceiling to see if he could remove a panel that might give him room to climb up. Maybe there would be an opening… a passage to climb through and out… or maybe… Suddenly the door swung open as a brief blast of air came through.

Joe thought that he had better get out while he had the chance. He got down off the chair and went for the door. *Since when would there be a blast of air coming from the hallway of the doctor's office?* As he opened the door further and stepped through, it was obvious that this was no longer the doctor's office. There was darkness and silence. The air was stagnant. Then suddenly, a young child came running toward him, shouting something in Japanese. Joe regained his focus and processed this information, translating the words in his head, and realized that the child had just said,"It's my turn!", as he ran through the door before the air pressure caused it to shut behind him.

"Where are you going?" Joe muttered, although the child was already long gone. He was met by several other children that seemingly didn't get their turn yet but were eager to get through as well. He tried the door, now from the opposite side, although he had no desire to step foot back in that room five but found that he was unable to open it. He began to ponder where he could be as he began to consider the significance of the note he had just read and recalled the old phrase *out of the frying pan and into the fire*.

Chapter Three

Joe looked around at the room that he had just entered. His eyes gradually adjusted to the dimness. It looked to him like the last glimmer of twilight before total darkness set in, although he was still inside a building. There were rows of desks facing a chalkboard. There were more children seated at several of the desks and others standing. Several of the children returned to their seats, appearing both fearful and disappointed. It looked like a classroom. He looked at a clock on the wall which read 8:16. So the clock was wrong because he knew it was about 3:30. Yet for some reason he felt like he was the only one who knew that. Were these children waiting for the teacher to arrive to start a new day? Except for the children muttering a few words to each other before quieting down, it was eerily quiet. There were no lights on and he began to wonder if there was any electrical power in the school. Were the kids being forced to sit in the dark? The only light that filtered in was from a set of windows on one side of the room, although all he could see from the windows was the brick wall of a neighboring building no more than ten feet away. He felt like it would be wrong to open a window for air, like it was supposed to be stuffy in there and he was out of place and didn't belong. He looked for a light switch on the wall, but without success. Just then he heard footsteps approaching rapidly. Three men entered the room.

"It happened so fast that we missed it," one of them said. "We never should have left the room."

"Did any of the children make it out?" another one of them asked.

"Well one child ran through the door to the patient waiting room when I came through," said Joe, "but it won't open now. He didn't pay me much attention, kind of like you… are doing."

"Are we too late?" the third one asked. The third man took out some type of electronic device as if he were scanning for lifeforms or something. He looked at a small screen, perhaps eight inches across, on the device, while moving an antenna from side to side. The device made sounds of varying pitch like some metal detector as various color patterns appeared on the screen.

"It's still active. It will open again, but that may be the last time, and our last chance to escape." He then looked directly at me. "You must be the fourth patient."

"Yes, I was just in the doctor's office. I was his fourth 3:30 appointment. But how would you know that? Don't tell me you're his first three patients and we all made the same mistake? And how did I end up in this school?"

"It isn't a school. It's an orphanage."

"Okay, so you know more about what's going on than me, but who are you?", Joe asked. This one looked like the leader of the group, the one who would have all the answers, if anyone did, so Joe directed his questions to him.

"I'm his brother, Micah. Perhaps you can notice the resemblance, even though it is obvious I'm the good looking one. And these are two of his patients that were just in the wrong place at the wrong time, Robert and Danny. So what do you have that we need?"

"I don't understand," said Joe. "I didn't plan on being here. I didn't volunteer for this. I've got things on my calendar to do. I have to get back."

"Didn't he fill you in? He frustrates me sometimes," said Micah. "My brother has a way of keeping important information to himself. You were chosen because of what you know or what you can do to get us out of here, obviously. He must have figured that you wouldn't go willingly, but he needed you. So, what did you tell Ben, my brother, that is?"

"We talked about my health… I guess the prognosis wasn't good… And my work. I don't think he was too impressed. I study ways to speed up space travel so we can get to other worlds. He seemed to joke about my speaking Martian."

"Well that won't help," said Micah. "Maybe if you spoke Japanese…"

"As a matter of fact, I do. Wait! I'm here because I speak Japanese?"

"You'll be able to communicate with the children," said Robert. "They are all Japanese."

"Like to ask them who is in charge of them?" asked Joe. "If none of you belong here, who is taking care of the children? Where are the adults, the workers in the orphanage?"

"We don't know," said Robert. "No adults were in the building."

"Come on guys," said Joe. "Do I have to be the one to figure it all out on my own?" Joe turned to one of the children and got down on his knees to talk to him face to face. "Otona." (adults) "Dokode." (where?) The child began to speak to him at what seemed a rapid pace to the other men listening. Joe and the child exchanged a few more words, then Joe stood up and turned to Micah.

"That was pretty good," said Micah. "I'm impressed!"

Joe looked at Micah with a mixture of anger and fear. "*What* is going on, here?"

"What did he say?" said Micah.

"Don't answer my question with a question," said Joe. "He said the adults went to the kitchen to get breakfast for them, just like any other morning. They would normally eat in here and the next room over. There is no separate dining room. But then they never came back. The children still haven't eaten. How long have they been waiting? Where is the kitchen?"

"There is no kitchen in this building," said Micah. "At least not anymore."

"Okay," said Joe. "Now it sounds like you're the one not filling me in. Perhaps you could start from the beginning and tell me what in the world is going on."

"Okay, I think you had better sit down for this. My brother discovered this portal from room five of his office about a week ago. Apparently, that was the first time it appeared. It was early in the morning and he was the first one in the office, as usual. He had just made his coffee and carried his cup with him as he drank it. He walked into room five and turned on the light. That was when the door shut behind him and he couldn't open it until it flew open a few minutes later on its own, but then it didn't lead back to the hallway of his office. It led him here. He checked to make sure that all he drank was coffee. Once he knew that wasn't the issue, he explored this whole building and met all the children. He doesn't speak a word of Japanese, so he couldn't really communicate with them very well. Then he realized where he was and that he had to find a way back and get the children out. But the portal had shut. He didn't know when or if it would open again, and there was nowhere else he could go. So, he waited and prayed and hoped for the best. Then finally the door opened just as suddenly as before and he walked through it and saw he was back in room five, and he thought that he could bring the children through as well, but after he walked into room five and two of the children followed, the portal shut again. He couldn't go back. But he knew what he had seen. He didn't dream it. It was real."

"I must admit that when he told me about it, I found it hard to believe," Micah continued. "He said that we should go back together and rescue the children, but we would need to find a way to keep the portal open long enough. But again the portal was closed and we had to wait for it to open again. We had no idea when that would happen. Two days later it opened again when I was in room five. But good ole Dr. Ben wasn't there at the time, so I came in alone. But then I couldn't get back. The portal opening was now too small in the opposite direction for me to get back, but large enough for a child to get through, so I sent one of the children through. But once one child went through, it closed and no one else could get through. I assumed she made it to the other side. But then I realized I was trapped here, with no way to get home. I figured Ben would figure out where I was. After all, he is the best doctor you'll ever meet, at least, that's the line he likes to use."

"There was a child in the waiting room yesterday with no parents," Joe recalled. "That must have been one of the children. And the one who ran through the door when I arrived was in a hurry to get through when it opened," Joe said and then paused in thought. "But why are they trying to get through? Does this have something to do with the disappearance of the adults? Don't the children belong here? They don't even understand what is on the other side of that door." Joe looked around again and back at the clock, which still said 8:16. "Looks like the power is out. It should be a little after 3:30."

"That may be the time in the doctor's office," said Robert. "But here it's 8:16. It's always 8:16."

"How can it always be 8:16? Time doesn't stand still. We're here talking. Time is moving. Something just killed the power at 8:16 when the adults disappeared, which means the children haven't eaten for hours."

"You said it was 3:30 at the doctor's office," said Danny. "What was the date?"

"It was Thursday, March 22, 2018. That was just a few minutes ago. That is still the date."

"I came through the portal on March 21," said Danny. "How can it already be the next day?"

"Was that you pounding on the door yesterday?"

"Yes, but it feels like I have only been here for half an hour or less, and the clock said 8:16 here when I arrived."

"I came through the portal on March 19," said Robert. "I had the same experience. It only seems like an hour or so has passed. I was just one of Ben's patients. I was trying to schedule an appointment on short notice, and as usual, he was booked solid. He scheduled me as the fourth patient at 2:30 on that day. He gave me this device you see me holding that turns out to be a magnetic field detector and can apparently sense displacements in time and space, if that makes any sense. It could detect this portal or wormhole that has been here all along but only on occasion opens enough to fit a person through. The doctor must have figured out from using this device when to expect the wormhole to open enough again for someone to fit through, and he scheduled me to go into room five as the fourth patient at that time. I should have known he couldn't see four patients at one time. He never schedules me as the fourth patient. He had no intentions of seeing me. He just wanted me to deliver this device through the portal so it could be used on this side."

"I also was the fourth patient," said Danny, "on March 21 at 4:30. The doctor must have obtained another device or figured out a pattern, because he knew when to expect the portal to open again."

"Why did he want you to come here?", asked Joe.

"Before I want in to room five, he gave me this small box containing medication and said to hold onto it and he would provide instructions for its use later. I got the impression that it was a prescription for me. So I hung onto it and when I came through the portal, also without a clue as to what I was getting into, I had it."

"What is it?" Joe asked.

"Potassium iodide."

"That's out of my field of expertise," said Joe.

"It treats radiation poisoning," said Danny. "The doctor was trying to buy time if he could keep us alive and get us all back through the portal before it would be too late. He knew when he examined the first child that they would need this. So, I believe this has helped us."

"And I came through on March 18," said Micah. "My brother came through on March 15 and was able to return. He thought he was gone for about ten or fifteen minutes, but when he returned it was the next day, March 16. He missed all his appointments for that day. That cost him a lot of money and left a lot of dissatisfied patients. But he didn't tell anyone about what had happened except for me. I mean, who would even believe this?"

"Well, he asked me about materials that protect against radiation," said Joe. "Since I work with materials to protect astronauts in space, this was something I was working on and the doctor wanted me to bring it when I came today. It opens up and acts as a shield against radiation."

"Yes," said Micah, "we will need that."

"Well, I sure hope we're not going into space today," said Joe, "but speaking of the day and your bizarre perceptions of time, I can say for a certainty that today is March 22, 2018. Look at my cell phone. You all have been here longer than you think."

"That's just based on the last satellite readings your phone was able to pick up," said Robert. "There are no satellites here, and that's not the date here. And the clock on the wall is correct. It has been the whole time we've been here."

"My brother had more confidence in you than you think," said Micah. "Do you study wormholes as a way to travel through space? Do you have some understanding of how they work?"

"Are you saying what we went through is a wormhole?", Joe asked. "That's impossible! A wormhole in the middle of San Francisco would destroy us all. There's nothing that could create or sustain that."

"Everything you just said is wrong," said Danny. "This is real. It is a portal, or wormhole, or whatever you want to call it. And we are not in San Francisco."

"Let me get this straight," said Joe. "We all go to the same doctor, Dr. Benjamin Gonzalez, and his office is in San Francisco, in Japantown. That's why the children speak Japanese. But if you expect me to believe that we went through a wormhole and are no longer on earth..." Joe just stopped in mid-sentence. He couldn't believe what he had just suggested. He looked around the dimly lit room. "I'm fairly certain we are still on earth. I'm breathing and feeling the normal balance of atmospheric pressure. I imagine we aren't far above sea level. And we don't have the technology to fake gravity that well to match earth. Whether this is a school or an orphanage, it's still on earth. So that can't be a wormhole."

"Really? Have you ever traveled through a wormhole before?"

"No, of course not."

"Have you ever seen one?"

"Not directly."

"So how can you say that's not a wormhole?"

"There's just no way a wormhole could form here. That would involve something catastrophic, something unheard of. It would even affect earth's orbit."

"Maybe you just don't have all the facts. A wormhole doesn't have to be that large. After all, we barely fit through it. To reply to your previous statements, yes, my brother Ben is the doctor and his office is in San Francisco, but no, that is not why the children speak Japanese," said Micah. "They have never been in San Francisco. Look around at where you are. Yes, we are still on earth, but take a closer look."

Joe strolled around the room. He saw a shelf with books, all in Japanese. "We've got to still be in Japantown. Maybe somehow in another building, but still in Japantown." Beside the chalkboard he saw the Japanese flag hanging, but it wasn't the flag that he would expect to see. "The Japanese flag should be the circle of the sun flag, but this was the rising sun flag. It was used only up to the Japanese surrender at the end of World War II. Is this history class?" Then he noticed the calendar. *August……. 1945?*

"This calendar was printed in Hiroshima, Japan. It's in remarkably good condition for being over 70 years old."

"How well do you know your history, Joe?", asked Micah. "You know Japanese, but what happened in August, 1945 in Hiroshima, Japan?"

"I know that history well. Doesn't everyone? The atomic bomb was dropped on Hiroshima, Japan on August 6, 1945."

"But how well do you really know your history?" said Robert. "At what time of day?"

"Well it was…" Joe paused as his face turned a pale shade of white, if there was such a shade. "At 8:16 a.m.?"

"So now you know where you are," said Danny. "At an orphanage in Hiroshima, Japan at 8:16 a.m., on August 6, 1945."

"Wait, Wait, Wait!" Joe shouted. "Are you telling me we went back in time, and now time is standing still…… at the *exact moment* the bomb exploded over Hiroshima?"

"Not exactly," said Micah. "The wormhole did carry us through both time and space so we did go back in time to the second that the atomic bomb exploded over Hiroshima, but when I arrived, the second hand on that clock was on the one. Now it's between the one and the two.

Two seconds have passed. So time is moving very slowly here, whereas several days have passed back home. As for our perceptions of time, that's all they are, *perceptions.* Only two seconds have actually passed here."

"We're like certain insects… the mayfly," said Robert. "Whose whole lifespan is only a day or maybe a few hours. Their perception of time is far different from a human or other creatures that live for decades or longer."

"So when that atomic bomb exploded," said Joe, "it must have disrupted space and time to such an extent to create this wormhole that comes out at the other end in San Francisco in 2018…. *I can't believe that human warfare has led to threatening the very fabric of space.* But time is still moving at some pace, although slowed, and conditions around us are changing rapidly, so this wormhole will collapse in seconds by that clock's time. Assuming we're close to ground zero… when that happens we're all dead."

"I'll just remove the battery or unplug it," said Danny.

"That won't help us," said Joe, not sure if Danny was ignorant or trying to lighten the mood, but there was no lightening this.

"If we really are that close to a nuclear explosion, how are we even alive?" asked Robert.

"There must be a pocket just within this building, like being trapped in a bubble, where time has been slowed to such an extent that we haven't felt the effects of the bomb yet," said Joe. "When we do, depending on our location in relation to that bomb, we'll either be instantly vaporized or exposed to a large amount of radiation. Apparently, based on the doctor's examinations, we are already exposed to some radiation."

"Yes, we are being affected," said Micah. "I've been here longer and I already feel the effects of the radiation. The children do as well. That was also apparent to my brother when he was here."

"That child I saw in the doctor's office," said Joe, "was sick with radiation poisoning. That must be it. How many children are in this building?"

"Right now there are forty two remaining," said Micah. "And you were sent to get them out."

"I may study wormholes, but how am I supposed to get them out?"

"With this!" said Danny. He handed Joe the device he was studying earlier when they first met him. "This device can detect the opening size and location of the portal by the contrasts in radiation of its location and the surrounding air. It's the location with the lowest radiation as air from 2018 flows through it to our contaminated air. But the doctor believes you can figure out a way for it to act as a brace to hold the portal open long enough and wide enough for us to get through if it opens again… I mean *when* it opens again."

Joe took a look at the device. He turned it in different directions and looked at it from various angles. "As a brace? Well, I can't jam it in the door to hold it open if that's what you mean. But *maybe…*" He pointed it toward the door where he entered and could still detect the wormhole. On the display it looked like different colors of light from 2018 bending as they made the trip through the wormhole back to 1945 Japan. Still, the opening was very small. "We can't do anything with an opening that small," Joe said in frustration. "This portal has to give me something to work with."

"Each time it opens enough for someone to pass through," said Micah, "it's for a shorter time and a smaller space. Based on the last readings we got, we believe we'll only get one more chance to get through, if you can widen the opening and hold it open longer. Can you modify the settings on that device to make that happen?"

"I can adjust the settings when I have a large enough opening to work with to create a magnetic field that will hold it open, that will in effect push the sides of it away from each other like magnets opposed to each other, but probably only for seconds before the magnetic field reverses and it collapses on itself, probably never to open again. That would also likely collapse this protective bubble that's keeping us alive. At that time I expect this building will be destroyed along with everything around it by the radiation and explosive power of the bomb. And having no concept of time, I don't know when the portal will open. We may only have seconds. How large is the area we can safely move within?"

"When my brother came in here," said Micah, "he explored this three-story building and all of its remaining rooms. If it had a kitchen, that part of the building was already gone, along with whoever was in there. He was able to see the slow-motion destruction happening outside, but apparently this time-space distortion only engulfed this building, so he realized he had better not try to open a door or window that led to the outside, which would probably be enough to disrupt the bubble and expose him to lethal radiation. But by the time I came, the third story was gone.... destroyed by the bomb."

"Now all that's left is the first floor," said Danny. "It's like the bubble is deflating. We're running out of space, *fast*."

"Micah, you said there were still 42 children here," said Joe. "I see maybe 25 or 30 here in this room. Where are the others, or is this all that is left?"

"Some are in the next room adjacent to this," said Micah. There's only one door out of this room, which leads to the hallway. Take a left out the hallway and it will be the next door on your left."

"I had better get the children in here," said Joe. "I can communicate with them the fastest and make them understand. You stay and watch the portal. This could soon be the last room left."

Joe raced out of the classroom and hurried out into the hallway, which was nearly pitch black, and to the next room in a search for every child he could find and gather back into the room. He recalled his history of what happened in Hiroshima. He knew if he didn't get the children through the portal, they likely wouldn't survive. But what if they did survive, or could survive? There were many children left orphaned in Hiroshima. Of those that survived the explosion, many children died later from the radiation. Others had nothing to eat and were desperate for whatever they could find or steal. Many of the girls were sold to the Yakuza organized crime syndicate into prostitution. They were the only ones who would give them anything. War had a way of tearing apart the fabric of society, and now even the fabric of space. This may have been the deadliest war on record, but it was also a time here in Hiroshima when the dead may have been better off than those who survived, but if he could get them through the portal and back to 2018…….. Joe knew he didn't have much time. *How do you even measure time when it is not moving at a reliable speed?* He began calling to the children wherever he saw them in the faint light to come and to hurry. "Kuru! Kuru! Isoide! Isoide!" He checked every remaining area in the building, just in case, and everyone rushed to the classroom.

"Time is speeding up!", said Micah. "While you were gone gathering the children, the clock advanced by two more seconds." Suddenly the glass of one of the windows in the room shattered in every direction and wind whistled through the openings into the room. It caused Danny to lose his footing and fall to the floor, even though he was the one who was the most buff of the group from his daily workout routine. "We need to seal that now!"

Joe reached for the material, which looked like a roll of thick fabric, that he brought at the doctor's request, that protects against radiation. "This will be plenty to cover it! Find some tape or nails or whatever we have to seal it and hold it in place!" Joe rushed over to the broken window and unrolled the fabric-like material that would shield out the radiation. Danny went over to hold the other end of it while Robert located some tape that would be strong enough to hold it in place.

As they were working frantically to secure that, they were well aware of the sounds of more of the building around them being torn apart. The sound was deafening. Debris was flying through the air in the hallway just on the other side of the door that Joe just brought the children through to get them all *safely* into the classroom, but now it wouldn't be safe to open that door. Obviously more of the building they were in was being destroyed by the bomb, and it seemed likely that this was the last room standing.

"Okay, I think that will hold…. *for now,*" said Robert. Just then a large chunk of metal nearly half the size of the classroom door came flying right through it from the hallway and just missed a couple of the children, while leaving a large hole in the door. That brought a measure of daylight into the room, which was a mixed blessing, because they could see better, but no, not really a blessing at all.

"We need to get that portal open somehow," said Micah, "and get out of here while we still can!"

"Bring me those scissors!" shouted Danny. "I need to cut the rest of this roll off so we can cover the door with the rest of it." Robert quickly grabbed the scissors and cut the roll away from the fabric that covered the window. He then ran across the room with it to what was left of the door. He quickly threw the remaining fabric over the gaping hole, but not before noticing that there was no hallway…. that there was *nothing*, on the other side of the door.

"This may be the world's first doomsday clock," said Joe. "It's moved another two seconds closer to our midnight…. Let me see that device again. Let's line up all the children so they are ready to go through the portal if….. no, *when* it opens. We're doing this!"

Joe then turned to each of the children. "Narabu! Narabu! (Line up) Koko ni! Koko ni! (Here)" Joe then looked for any fluctuations in the radiation readings in the air between them and the way back to room five….. *and survival.* He focused in on the spot with the least radiation. Suddenly the door leading to room five opened slightly. There was now an opening in the portal.

"The wormhole has opened just barely," said Joe. "I may be able to modify the magnetic field just enough with this device…." Beads of sweat rolled down Joe's face. His hands were shaking. This event wasn't on his calendar. He wasn't supposed to be here. This defied all logic. *I can't do this. It will never work. No, I must…* modify it just enough to expand it sufficiently…. to get us all through. To fit through one person at a time…. But then once it collapses and closes in on itself it will never open again. *Not to mention the fact that this room won't be here much longer either.* Joe adjusted several settings on the device to find what would have the desired effect.

By now it sounded like they were in a tornado. They were hearing debris of various sizes striking the exterior walls of all sides of the room as well as the ceiling above. Not only were Joe's hands shaking, but the entire room was shaking. The clock knocked back and forth and fell off the wall. Joe's last-ditch efforts finally got the wormhole to open wider. "Go now!" Joe shouted. "Send the children in a line, one at a time. That's all that will fit."

The children disappeared one by one into the wormhole. Chunks of debris from the remains of nearby buildings continued to bombard the exterior walls of their classroom, that by now were all exposed to the outside. This was the last room left standing in the building. It became apparent that much of the wall behind the chalkboard was gone when they could hear debris striking not the wall but the back of the chalkboard. The children continued passing through the wormhole until all of them were through and now stood just Robert, Danny, Micah and Joe. Joe struggled to hold the wormhole open. As the last few children were making their way through Joe began to realize what the doctor's true intent was. He didn't send Joe in to *save* the children. He sent Joe in to *die* for the children. It occurred to him only now that there was no way for him to enter the wormhole while also using the device to keep the wormhole open. The device had to stay on *this* side to keep the wormhole open. He couldn't just let go of the device and leap through as the wormhole would instantly close once he released the controls on the device.

"Joe, you did it!", said Micah. "They made it! It's still wide enough for us to make it. Let's go!"

Joe paused for a second and looked back at Micah. "No. I'm sorry," said Joe sadly. "*Someone* has to stay behind. The wormhole won't stay open on its own, and I can't walk through holding this device. It has to stay on this side of the wormhole with me holding the controls to keep the portal open…" Joe took another good look at the three remaining men. He spoke up again, "*I'll* stay. I don't have long to live anyway. The doctor said so. *You* need to go. This portal will collapse in seconds, and the room is falling apart around us."

"You can still make it!", said Robert. "You can back in and hold the device on this side of the wormhole and leap through as you release it."

"That won't work. Even that fraction of a second will cause it to collapse on me."

"I should be the one to stay!", said Micah. "I came in here knowing what I was getting into. You're an innocent victim that had no choice."

"No, if you had wanted to volunteer, you should have done so before I took control of this device. It's too late. I can't let go of the controls to get out now anyway. If I try to pass the controls to you, the portal will shut. Please go now. It's now or we all die. The pressure is about to overpower the magnetic field and reverse it, locking us in here. There's nothing else I can do to stop it."

Suddenly an explosion destroyed the entire wall behind the chalkboard and pieces of the chalkboard came flying toward the four of them. A few good-sized pieces went flying right into the wormhole. Heat, radiation and debris poured into the classroom as they now had a view outside of the ruin around them. "Go now!", said Joe. "Get everyone out of room five and as far away as possible! Evacuate the doctor's office!"

Robert, Micah and Danny each went through the portal, one by one. Joe now remained, looking into the wormhole but unable to enter, alone at ground zero in Hiroshima, Japan on August 6, 1945 at 8:16 a.m., recalling the events of this day as well as the day for him that started in 2018, the day that would be his last. His whole life flashed before him as he realized how so much of his focus was all about himself, that there were so many missed opportunities where he could have made a difference in the lives of others, and he wondered what he had really accomplished with his life. Then he realized what he had just done. He just saved 45 people that would have died in 1945. He did make a difference. But why did it take until he knew he was dying anyway to think about others ahead of himself? Why couldn't he have been more selfless throughout his life? He was contemplating what the last few seconds of his life really meant when the force of the explosion with time now moving forward at normal speed blew him and the device right into the wormhole. The wormhole collapsed immediately. The atomic bomb quickly vaporized the entire orphanage as it had already everything else around it, and no one still living in 1945 would have any idea that an atomic explosion created a wormhole into the future that saved the lives of dozens of children.

Chapter Four

Back in the doctor's office the date was now March 23, 2018. The explosion caused radiation and debris to come flying through the wormhole and it destroyed practically everything in room five as well as most of the doctor's office. Those few seconds Joe spent thinking about his own mortality on the other side of the wormhole amounted to close to an hour on this side, and the men who came through along with the doctor had proceeded to evacuate the entire office. They were all standing outside in front of the office when they all heard the booming sound of the explosion and witnessed the cloud of dust and fire that followed. They worked frantically to put out any fires that had started.

Most people in the area would just think that it was a gas explosion or an unfortunate accident. They would later hear reports on the news to that effect. The truth wouldn't be reported to the general public. It would be too hard for people to accept, despite the dozens of survivors that could tell their stories. They weren't ready to believe that such a thing were possible. They preferred to go about their daily lives, eating and drinking, buying and selling, as if everything was just as it was before, as if this miracle never happened. They would just dismiss the rumors and stories they would hear. Life would go on.

Of course, there would be an investigation into the cause of the explosion. The doctor would be thoroughly questioned as well as others present at the time. They would check the wiring and gas lines in the building. The insurance company would come up with multiple reasons not to pay for the damage. In the end it would just be left unresolved, and no criminal charges would be filed against the doctor. Any radiation detected in the area would be blamed on faulty or outdated medical equipment. But the media would quickly move on to something else, and this story would be forgotten.

Their day wasn't over. In the short time they had spent together, Micah, Robert, Danny and Joe, not to mention the doctor, had a unique shared experience. They weren't sure how much radiation they had been exposed to, or how this would affect them in the future, but they didn't just want to walk off and go home and never see each other again. Besides that, there was still one question left unanswered. Micah and the others had to know what had happened to Joe. They had to make some attempt to find him.

With the children all safely removed from the area, Micah and the doctor attempted to go back in the building to inspect the rooms and to search for Joe. As they opened the front door and entered the waiting room, it resembled a war zone, which, in fact, it really was. How do you explain that the effects of an atomic bomb dropped on Japan over 70 years ago has now left damage in San Francisco in 2018? War was and still is a terrible thing. Man's inhumanity to man had been evident throughout history. This just served as another reminder of that. No one would be waiting in this waiting room for some time.

As they made their way through the waiting room and down the hall, it looked eerily similar to the orphanage they left behind in Japan. There was darkness, debris, smoke and ash. Room five and room four were now one open area of desolation. There was no longer the smell of cotton balls or mothballs, just what the fire and smoke had left behind. It was difficult to breath, and it occurred to them that perhaps they should get out of here. Then in the darkness they saw Joe's body. The blast actually returned him back to 2018 where he could at least have a decent burial.

"Joe said he was very sick," said Micah, "that he didn't have much time to live, and he chose to die so we could live. He had the knowledge to control the wormhole with that device, he was able to speak Japanese to communicate with the children, and since he had a short time to live anyway, he was ready to die for something meaningful. I can't believe you found the perfect person to come through the portal to save us."

"I didn't, Micah… But I was running out of time, and I needed to find someone. He just had to believe that he was that person. You see, Joe was in near perfect health. He probably had 40 years to live."

"So, you lied to him. What about your oath as a doctor to preserve life?"

"I did preserve life. The lives of those 42 children and the three of you. You see, someone had to die, and having to make a split-second decision, it would be a lot easier to make that decision to die for them if he thought he was going to die soon anyway after returning."

"If I had known that Ben, I would have stayed in his place."

"I know. That's why I couldn't allow you to know."

"He didn't deserve to die! Is my life more valuable than his, just because I'm your brother?"

"To me it is. That's a benefit that comes from being family." Just then in the darkness they detected a movement from Joe and realized he was still breathing.

"He's alive!", said Micah. Joe coughed and opened his eyes. He caught his breath and looked up and saw Micah and Ben standing there.

"Where am I?", he asked. "When am I?"

"Joe," said the doctor, "you are back in my office in San Francisco, yes, in 2018, a day after you left. You did it! You saved them all! Exactly as I planned it. I can see the headlines reporting how we saved all these lives. My office may just be closed for a while for repairs."

"What?" Joe reacted, stunned to look around and see the office in a shambles. "I can't believe it! I thought you sent me in there to die… But I found out something about myself, something I wish I had learned a long time ago. I really never sacrificed myself for others like that until I realized I had nothing to lose anyway. I would have lived my life a lot differently if I had realized what it really means to come to the rescue for others…. It is so hard to just realize that *now…*" He said with a sigh… "at the end. So give it to me straight doc… How much time do I have?"

"Well Joe," the doctor responded, "you were exposed to a lot of radiation in there, and you almost died getting thrown back through the wormhole. You may have some broken bones. But, barring any unforeseen calamity that may befall you, I'd say you have as much as 40 years ahead of you. You are as healthy as a horse, and I'm not talking about the ones they have to take out and shoot. You are in great shape, although you are not as buff as Danny."

"But your note! You said…"

"My note worked exactly as planned," said the doctor. "*Better* than planned. Look what you accomplished! No prescription could have accomplished that."

"I can't believe it! So, what do I do now?"

"We'll patch you up, once you are recovered you can help with the children, and I'll see you for your next checkup in one year, as the first patient. But you'll always be the fourth patient to me.

MARTIAN TIME

by James Hart

Prologue

July 20, 2031 1:17 p.m. Local Time (20:17 UTC)

"Three, two, one, ignition and liftoff." The sound was deafening to those gathered around in the New Mexico desert as the rocket lifted off. Still, it was quite a sight to behold, one that had to be experienced in person to be truly appreciated. It was exactly 62 years to the minute of the Apollo 11 touchdown on the moon, just as planned. Of course, it was also the anniversary of the day in 1976 when Viking I became the first spacecraft to land successfully on Mars. However, this was not just *any* rocket shooting through the atmosphere. It was carrying a nuclear missile. Many wondered if this was a good idea. It left many governments wondering if this *really was* a peaceful mission, as the rocket sped higher in the atmosphere over North American soil. If it was to fall back to earth, the results could be disastrous. But it continued accelerating on its upward course and soon left the atmosphere altogether, on its way to an interception with an asteroid, which was only the stuff of fictional movies and stories a few decades ago. A group of scientists had wondered for some time if exploding a nuclear missile on or near an asteroid could alter its course. Taking the lead in this endeavor was Mr. Joe Schmoe, President of Mission Control, with its headquarters in the San Francisco Bay Area. Joe really did believe that space was the final frontier where great treasures were waiting to be discovered. This one particular asteroid was not coming especially near earth, and certainly not a danger to anyone, but it was large enough and on a path that a rocket could intercept, so it could serve as a good test. As it was, this nuclear missile was nearing its expiration date and the current administration had the "use it or lose it" mentality, so they found a way to use this nuclear missile in peacetime, if you classify having a force field between Russia and Alaska to keep anything from crossing through as being peacetime. Still, since this was an unmanned rocket, the course and timing had to be just right for the explosion to have any affect. It would be several months before it would reach the asteroid.

During the course of those months, the rocket was monitored closely to ensure that when it reached its destination it made contact with the asteroid rather than have a near miss and explode out of range. It stayed on course and arrived according to schedule. Finally, once arriving and making contact, the missile exploded. The Hubble Plus Verizon space telescope sent back vivid images in 10K.

Of course, Joe Schmoe and his staff at Mission Control were ready and eager to declare victory. Any declared victory would lead to more funding for future missions. "Did it work, Joe? Was the mission successful?" asked his Operations Officer, Steve. Joe often referred to Steve as his young apprentice. Steve was 30 years younger than Joe, and he was sharp as a whip. That along with Joe's experience made for a great team.

"We'll see. A probe is on its way. We'll see what that reveals." Joe had nothing else to say about the probe and refused to discuss *the incident.* On the night before the probe was to be launched, someone gained unauthorized access to the launch area and painted on the side of the probe the letters V-G-E-R in permanent ink. Well, it was too late to clean it off and still make the launch window (yes, there is always a launch window), so the decision was made, against Joe's better judgment, to just leave it. For weeks after that, Joe got a barrage of, "C'mon Joe, what's the worst that could happen?" He finally sent down an executive order never to speak of this again, realizing that people have short memories and would soon forget. He may one day find that he wished people had better memories, but that is yet to come.

Chapter 1

Arrival

The crew awoke from sleep, unaware of how long they had been out. It was eerily silent. Captain Dave Whitney was in command here. He was 41 years old, six foot two inches tall, solidly built, quite sure of himself and was everything an astronaut should be, at least according to the academy. He met the textbook definition of captain, guaranteeing the mission would be a success. He scanned his surroundings, trying to recall his last move. He wasn't in the sleeping chamber but sitting in his captain's chair. Something just didn't feel right. They hadn't made him Admiral yet. No, that wasn't it. He turned his head to look toward his first mate, Kate, who happened to be his wife. Kate was 39 years old, five foot four inches tall, also solidly built and everything an astronaut should be, or she wouldn't be here, and neither would Dave. When Dave was so sure of himself, she had to be sure that she could feel sure about whether what he was sure about was a sure thing. They were perfect for each other. Kate was sitting in the chair beside him. Her eyes were closed. Dave, despite his rugged exterior, spoke softly to her, as well he should. "Kate… Kate…" Kate raised her head and opened her eyes, then closed them again as if it were too bright for her right now. Dave repeated, "Kate… Kate…"

"I've got a headache!" came her snappy reply.

Undeterred, Dave continued. "We're not home. We're in space, remember? Are we still on autopilot?"

Kate opened her eyes once again, becoming fully aware of where they were, not in their home or even on earth. "Oh. Well, my headache is clearing up, thank God." They were in fact tens of millions of miles from earth, with Mars looming before them. Kate leaned forward and checked the control panel. The normal array of lights were flickering on and off in silence as the ship's computer monitored everything from the temperature and oxygen level in the room to their heart rates and breathing. "Yes, we are still on autopilot, but something is wrong. We're heading *away* from Mars. We're on the edge of the Martian atmosphere. How could we have slept through that? The last thing I remember… What is the last thing I remember?" They had spent a long time in space, with so much reliance on their ship's navigation system that the government boasted was flawless, or actually *unsinkable* was the word they were using. Was their fatigue starting to show? Were their minds being affected by the long trip in space? They did their best to keep their minds and bodies active, following a predetermined plan of regular exercise as well as mental challenges aboard ship. For months they were drawing ever closer to the red planet. All of a sudden, it seemed to be right upon them, yet somehow they were off course.

"Whatever happened, the only way to land on Mars now is to switch to manual." Of course, Dave had only performed this type of landing in the simulator. He was successful 70% of the time, just enough to graduate from the academy, and that was while being graded on a curve, which many felt was a bad idea. He never thought he would actually be doing this for real, since everything was typically automated. If he could pull this off, they would *have* to make him Admiral. Of course, being the Captain, he never gave any hint that he had any doubt about whether this would be successful. If he was going to one day be an Admiral, he had to act like an Admiral now. He took a deep breath in the dead silence. Then he uttered the words that he thought would later be written forevermore in the history books: "Switching to manual." He imagined documentaries about Mars being broadcast into the 22nd century and beyond, sounding something like: *and the only way they were able to land safely on Mars was after Admiral David Whitney uttered those famous words: "Switching to manual."* Of course, everyone watching the documentary would repeat those words as they were being spoken, or at least move their lips in sync with them, wishing no doubt that *they* could be so famous. People would line up for autographed copies of his story, "Switching to Manual" with his picture on the cover, showing his left side, because that was his best side.

He flicked the switch to manual, causing some awkward shifting in the ship's position as he got the feel of the controls, which for some reason, perhaps because of the actual mass of the ship, felt far more sensitive than in the simulator. But then why shouldn't it, when the lives of his entire family hung in the balance! He would be sure to note this concern in the captain's log. Each day he made several entries into the captain's log, not always sharing the contents with his family. For example, he documented when the ship's automatic sensors avoided debris in space while the others were sound asleep. He didn't want to concern his family about the number of close calls along the way. Who would have thought that space would have so much stuff in it? It was all that dark matter people knew was out there but couldn't see, matter usually too small to reflect much light. He sarcastically noted about how the ship's unsinkable navigation system saved them again. He never really trusted anything that was *that* automated. Nothing beats what the human eye can see, along with his quick thinking of course. Kate kept her own log too, since she assumed Dave would miss many important details she would want to remember, such as the time Kristy took some of Brandy's food ration, thinking she wouldn't notice. Oh, she noticed! That was the first sibling fight in zero gravity. Fortunately, the ship was able to hold together through it. Some pieces of dried scrambled eggs may still be floating about the ship.

Speaking of siblings, about this time the teenage girls had awoken and came to see what all the commotion was about. "Dad, what are you doing?" asked Kristy, their 17-year-old daughter. "You don't play video games. You had better let me land it." Kristy really didn't think of him as the captain. To her he was just dad. Hopefully in a life and death situation she would be trusted to follow the captain's orders, should such a situation arise. But for now she was just a teenager living the dream of being as far from earth as anyone had ever traveled, and she wasn't dead yet. That's always a plus.

"Trust me. I've got this," said her dad as he single-handedly steered the ship around back in the direction needed to enter the Martian atmosphere. As soon as he had them traveling back toward Mars, a warning alarm sounded. "What's that all about? I can make a course correction anytime I want!" Dave didn't need a navigational system finding fault with him. He was thinking of shutting those pesky alarms off altogether.

Just then though, something ominous came into view. "There seems to be some sort of cloud ahead," said Kate. "I'm scanning it now. The computer advises we use caution. It's detecting unusually high levels of radiation." As Kate stared into it, it appeared as if it were generating its own weather, but how was that possible? There were flashes of light within it in all directions that looked like lightning, and even a variety of colors that just didn't seem to fit in here in space. "Should we send a message to Mission Control? After all, the Martian atmosphere shouldn't even support a cloud of this size, and we can't steer around it."

Dave, of course, had an answer for this. "Kate, being this far from earth, Mission Control can only do so much for us. It will take at least 15 minutes for a message to reach them and another 15 minutes after they send us a reply for us to receive it. Besides that, our fuel reserves are a bit lower than they calculated for us to have at this point in the journey. I'll be sure to have a talk with their mathematicians about that. For us to hold our position and wait for a reply when they won't be able to tell us what it is anyway seems counterproductive. We're in the best possible position to evaluate this ourselves. This is one of those quick decisions we must make on our own. This is the sort of thing we trained for." Dave prided himself on his ability to think on his toes and make quick decisions. Everyone else should get on board with his thinking as well. True, the training was time consuming and expensive, so they had to prove that after all those hours of training they knew what they were doing rather than just being able to answer questions on an exam.

"Well, it doesn't appear very threatening to me," said their younger daughter Brandy, only 15 years old presently, and just 14 years old when they left earth, making her the youngest person ever to be in space. Before leaving earth, she was asked hundreds of times what it felt like to be the youngest person in space. She usually said something to the effect that she had no idea what it felt like since she hadn't been in space yet, but when she got really annoyed with it, she said something like, "I don't know. What's it like to be so ugly?" She just wanted to speak her mind rather than be told that she had to be an example for other young impressionable minds out there thinking about their future. If they wanted an impression, she would give them one.

She kept her hair short because she didn't want to have to mess with it and because she wanted to look different from her sister. Yet, no matter how different she looked, there would always be someone who would say to her, "Are you Kristy or Brenda? I always mix you two up." The answer usually was, "No. And it's Brandy, like a shot of Brandy, which is what you're about to get from me." She would look for opportunities, though, to put on some of her mom's makeup when she wasn't looking. Her mom would tell her she was too young for that and didn't need makeup anyway. "How am I ever going to get a boyfriend if I can't wear makeup?"

Her mom would tell her, "You're beautiful just the way you are."

"Are you saying I'm beautiful on the inside, because that's not good enough."

"Sweetie, what I am saying is that a boyfriend who is only attracted by your makeup is not a boyfriend you want." But then, once they were chosen for the mission and were on camera constantly, they were all wearing makeup, even dad, to take that glare off his forehead. He didn't even have a choice in the matter. The lawyers said that if someone were blinded by the glare from his forehead and sued Mission Control, the mission would be scrapped.

She continued her response to her father, "It looks like those cumulus clouds we learned about in school. Just a fair-weather thing."

"My thoughts exactly!" said Dave, surprised that he actually agreed with Brandy. "Let's forge on ahead and get to the surface where our comfortable Martian habitats are waiting for us." Dave said this realizing full well the habitats were not going to be that comfortable, which is why Brandy brought her pillow from home. She wasn't sure how the reduced gravity would affect the comfort from her pillow. Probably it would just expand outward with less atmospheric pressure pushing on it from the outside, making it even fluffier. No doubt there would be much about Mars that would lack the comforts they were accustomed to at home. All of this was taken into consideration when planning the first human Mars mission. Since loneliness could be a big factor, it was determined that a family would be sent, since these would be people who were used to living together and loved and trusted each other. Of course, each one would have to be eager to be a part of the mission for it to be successful. David Whitney was the type of man who could make quick decisions without having all the facts, which could be necessary on a journey like this, though possibly deadly. It was a very delicate balance. He worked with Joe Schmoe at Mission Control from the beginning of the planning stage for this mission, even as his daughters were growing up. His wife Kate had likewise been involved with the planning for many years and sharing information with their daughters to build their excitement for an eventual mission. They also had to understand the risks, aware that they had their whole lives ahead of them. So, everyone was on board and went through the entire training program at the academy. Now they saw their destination, Mars, so close ahead of them.

Captain Dave took them through the cloud and they barely noticed the turbulence. Okay, it was a bit bumpy, but it could have been worse. "Okay, we're ready to separate from the rest of the ship to move on to our landing, so here goes nothing." With a flick of a switch, their ship separated into its two parts, sending the larger portion into orbit around Mars while they continued on toward the surface in the lander, just as expected. Remaining in orbit would be not just the heavier portion of the ship, but also their supplies for the return trip to earth. The orbiter was fully automated and required no pilot. Landing on Mars with as little as possible would reduce the amount of fuel needed to take off again. It was vital that they conserve supplies wherever possible to allow for the unexpected. "Expect the unexpected," they often told their girls. Kristy was quick to point out that if they were expecting it, it wouldn't be unexpected. "Wow! That was unexpected, which was exactly what I was expecting." Her dad told her that that was the whole point, so you would be prepared for anything. Kristy also decided that somehow, someway, she was going to be the game changer on this trip. Her long, straight, flowing hair that came down to just above her waist made her known as the woman with the longest hair in space, and that was finally inserted into the record books. She always had long hair, and all through her years at the academy, she would often hear, "Don't operate heavy machinery with that hair." Her hair would usually get caught somewhere as she was taking off or putting on her spacesuit. Still, it was such a part of her that she could never see cutting it shorter. She would enjoy tossing her hair behind her in slow motion and telling people, "I do shampoo commercials."

Actually, it paid off because she did get hired to do shampoo commercials. "People envy my hair. You wish you had my hair." Her signature was flashed across the label of every bottle of her brand of shampoo. Everyone's signature was a sign of who they were, although it looked nothing like their names since cursive writing was no longer being used. It was something uniquely theirs, since before it could be approved it had to be run through the worldwide database to make sure it wasn't already taken.

"One night when you're sleeping, I'm going to cut that hair off," said Brandy. Of course, she didn't mean it, but liked saying it anyway, just to keep her sister at bay.

Some really clever scientists on earth had worked all of the foreseeable scenarios of this trip out in advance, though Dave didn't really trust them. *Could they really understand all the variables this far from earth? Could they really account for things like, "If you girls don't quiet down back there, I'll turn this ship around right now!"*

"Can you see the landing area down there?" asked Kate, as she strained herself to get a good look out of the viewport, a small round window like that on an airplane, just for viewing, not for opening.

"I'm sure we're close," said Dave. "We may have drifted off course a bit, having to switch to manual, so we may have to walk to reach the drop off point where the supplies were delivered for us over the last few years. A nice big X on the ground would have been nice, but we'll have to make the best of it."

"I heard that X marks the spot," said Kristy, with a snicker.

"Well, they sure came in handy several years ago when I was doing survey work with my drone," said Dave. "But I gave that all up to be an astronaut." Yes, like George Washington and Abraham Lincoln, David Whitney had been a land surveyor before moving on to other things, so he imagined he would be grouped with them in the history books.

Regardless of the few bumps along the way, nothing could take away from their excitement at this moment when they were about to be the first people to land on Mars. Joe Schmoe and his staff had worked hard for many years back at Mission Control in San Francisco to make this mission possible. Although Joe had not been able to cut the travel time to 30 days as he had wished, this trip was made in seven months, the fastest ever. Sure, it wasn't perfect. There were setbacks as well as mistakes that were swept under the rug before they could catch the attention of the media. Yet there were also deadlines to meet, or others may have beaten them to this place, and that just couldn't be allowed to happen. Deadlines have a way of making things happen, for better or for worse. Now, they were here. The risks had been worth it. No one would question that. They would be the first ones on Mars and that would be documented in the history books forevermore. First, of course, they had to safely land manually on the surface, or at least get close enough for the ship's sensors to land it in place. Captain Dave maneuvered the ship into position and landed safely on the planet, ready to have his picture plastered on the digital cover of Time magazine. (They still *called* it a magazine, although it was just a website.) Maybe they would even do a rare special paper edition, even if that meant they had to cut down some extra trees to do it, after congress put it to a vote. After all, this was history in the making.

Chapter 2

Missing

Joe Schmoe arrived at Doctor Gonzalez' office in Japantown in San Francisco. The fog had lingered all day, making it feel quite chilly on this summer day. He was starting to feel it in his bones, even with his jacket zipped up and the hoodie tied over his head. As he was approaching his sixty fifth birthday, it was time for another checkup. He entered the waiting room, twice the size it was before it was destroyed from an explosion carried from the past through a wormhole, an event Joe would never forget. Wormhole damage wasn't covered in the doctor's insurance on his property, so the doctor had to pay out of his own pocket to make the repairs. Now he understood how his uninsured patients felt.

Joe wanted to make sure he got in for his 4:00 p.m. appointment before what he assumed would be two other patients who would also be scheduled for 4:00 p.m., so he arrived at 3:52 p.m. "Hello Joe," said Sarah, the receptionist. "Go ahead and have a seat in the waiting room."

Joe nervously looked at the clock and went over in his head how this would all play out, from his seating in the waiting room long enough to see an entire episode of whatever crime drama was showing on the television to the next wait in the patient room to that drive home in his car as a real driver and all the driverless vehicles surrounding him, judging him. He knew that if he ever was in an accident, it would be determined he was to blame, since driverless vehicles don't make human mistakes and he was one of the last holdouts in the Bay Area still driving his car manually. But that's a subject for another time.

As he looked at the cracked upholstery of the chair he was about to sit in, trying to avoid the sharp edges, the receptionist spoke to him again. "Joe, excuse me, I have to ask you. I just can't stop thinking about it."

Joe turned his head slowly her way, opening his mouth, although nothing came out for three seconds while a hundred possible questions flashed through his brain until he had determined the most likely one to come. "Go ahead Sarah. What is it?"

"What's up with your name, Joe Schmoe? You know, that's not normal. Where did that come from?"

Joe rolled his eyes. *That* question again! He had nailed it. This time he would use it to his advantage. "If I give you the short version, can you promise to get me into the doctor with no delays?"

She smiled back at him, mostly because he reminded her of her grandfather. "You got it, Mr. Schmoe."

Now he just felt old, which indeed he was, but proceeded nonetheless with his explanation. "My mother was Italian and wanted to name me Giuseppe and didn't realize my father's last name was pronounced "Ssshmoe" and thought it was pronounced "shhmooooey". My father thought that her pronunciation of his last name was her pet name for him so that is how I became Joe Schmoe."

She looked at him with a classic clueless look, and then moved on. "Okay, a promise is a promise," she muttered.

"What does that mean?"

"The doctor will see you for your 4:00 appointment in a few minutes. You can go into room number three." Joe thanked Sarah for keeping her word and headed for the room to await the doctor. All the other rooms were in use, so the doctor was certainly keeping busy. The room looked much as he had remembered it from previous visits. There was the examining table and *two* chairs since there would never be a need for more than two people to sit down at the same time in this room. The doctor or nurse could sit in one chair while the patient sat in the other while they discussed vital statistics or maybe the Giants game from last night. If the patient brought a family member, that person would have to stand and be grateful they were even allowed in. The wallpaper was faded and hadn't been replaced in at least 30 years because despite his success, the doctor didn't like to spend money. Newer doctors' offices had installed digitizers that flashed digital wallpaper on the walls and could be changed or rotated regularly, but not this doctor.

On the back of the door was the food pyramid to keep patients distracted while waiting for the doctor, since no one could really figure out the food pyramid anyway. Was this the revised food pyramid from 2025, or one of those outdated food pyramids still in circulation for some reason? It did look rather worn and faded, but that didn't answer the question in Joe's mind. Some countries had even replaced the food pyramid with a food octagon, but that's another story. The doctor did provide free WiFi now, since he no longer carried paper copies of magazines, and maybe because it was provided free by the City and County of San Francisco to everyone. That provision didn't make a lot of sense, since he always wanted you to turn your cell phone off to prevent someone from having a heart attack or something. In a few minutes, Doctor Gonzalez walked into the room to greet him.

"Hello Ben," said Joe.

"Good to see you again Joe," said the doctor. "It's been at least a year since your last visit. I think you just may live to be 90, like I predicted. I hope I'm around to see that come true."

"Well, you are the best doctor I'll ever meet, like you enjoy saying. I suppose that's why I keep coming, or maybe it's for these informative medical newsletters that I can access online at home anyway."

"I'm pretty sure it's the former. Obviously, my subliminal messages are working. It somewhat surprises me to see you here for a checkup on this day of all days. You've been in the news a lot lately, what with that mission to Mars of yours. Your job is not so top secret anymore. I try to follow the news, but you know how busy I am. Did you make contact with the landing party? I've been swamped all day, but I'm hearing a lot of talk from my patients. One of my 2:00 appointments even cancelled because he was too busy following the story, but I had two others scheduled at the same time anyway, so I barely noticed."

"I can't explain it doc. They were expected to land on Mars around 3:00 a.m. our time. I was up all night. Our last communication from them was received at 2:58 a.m., so it would have been sent at 2:42 a.m. At that point everything was going well, right on schedule. They were soon to land. We have not been able to reach them since, now over 13 hours."

"What about the rovers on the surface? They are still functioning, right? My taxpayer money is paying for them."

"They really only cost you about three cents a month, but yes, we're still receiving feed from them. We can see the landing area where the autopilot should have placed them. The strange thing is, it has not picked up *anything*. If they landed or crashed, it was somewhere out of our view, but if they did land safely, why haven't they contacted us or responded to our messages? As you might say, the diagnosis is not good. It's as if they never landed at all."

The doctor reflected on the possibilities. "Perhaps they landed out of sight and temporarily lost the ability to communicate."

"I hope that's all it is. All this stress is not good for me."

"Joe, you're in *great* health, even with that stressful job of yours," said the doc. "Now that you are 65, it looks like you're in the Medicare system. You just have to select which part from Part A to Part ZZ that you will use. It's easy to choose. Just answer the 500-question survey to know what is best for you. You can even have your robotic assistant do it for you. Since he's connected to the internet, he fills it out live as you answer."

"Doc, you know I don't use those robotic assistants."

"Once you get on Medicare, you can practically get your robot for free. Otherwise, you'll have to get your kids to take care of you in your old age, and like yourself, fewer people are having kids nowadays, which also explains why earth's population has leveled off, but I digress."

"Well, the way I am going, I'm just going to stay active until I die. Fewer people are active nowadays too, so *they* can use those robots. I just don't want a robot that may get hacked by the Russians and turn against me."

"I would consider that highly unlikely. They would have to steal all of your fingerprints and your retina scan to pull that off. Now that people are getting their fingerprints replaced every two years, we're always ahead of the hackers. You *are* getting your fingerprints changed every two years, *right*? Unless you have a criminal record in which case you must keep your old fingerprints for life. Anyway, all that aside, if you are in good health, at your age I recommend yearly checkups. It will help us detect any small problems before they become big problems. Sometimes you may feel fine but something is still going on. It will also improve my bottom line.”

“Of course. Let me ask you something doc. You never saw anything from that wormhole after what happened fifteen years ago? After all, you’re the one that got me into that mess.”

“No. I still have the device that was able to detect the time-space displacement. I couldn’t really throw that out. It’s a great conversation piece. Of course, if I try to tell people the truth about what happened, they think I’m crazy, even though the children we rescued have grown up and are living productive lives. I still get visits from them. Anyway, it never picked up any other signs of a wormhole. Do you believe it should have?”

“I really didn’t expect it to, but I figured if it happened here, it just has me wondering if this type of thing could be more common than we know. So, I constructed a better quality device, using our research budget of course, and had it sent up into space on a satellite with a telescope in orbit, just because I could. It’s been up there over a year and has not detected anything, which I suppose isn’t surprising. It’s like searching for a needle in a haystack anyway.”

“In my experience,” said the doc as he was shining his stethoscope, “there is usually a needle in there somewhere, and if you’re persistent enough, you’ll find it, even though you’ll likely be poked in the process.”

“Is that some sort of veiled warning?”

"Actually, I thought I was being quite direct. Just make sure you're searching in the right haystack. Some of these parallel haystacks all look the same, that is, if you believe in parallel haystacks. By the way, whatever happened on your mission to save the earth from an asteroid?"

"Well doc, I believe we got the probe to the right place, but we can't seem to locate the asteroid at all."

"Wow, it seems like you're losing a lot of your things. How about I loan you my GPS device, the one with the digital assistant that has an English accent? He can find anything."

"I'm serious, doc. It couldn't have completely destroyed it. We have the arrogance to think our rockets and weapons are so powerful, but compared to what's out there in space, we're just a drop from a bucket."

"Maybe it was like one of those lava rocks. Those are pretty lightweight. A nuclear missile could destroy one of those."

"I don't think so, doc."

"Well Sherlock, remember once you eliminate the impossible, whatever remains, no matter how improbable, must be the truth."

"Then I might just have to burst some bubbles and reveal the truth."

"Oh, yeah, well, the truth is out there."

"Doc, you're just throwing all of your quotes at me today like you're the expert."

"I can't argue with that logic, but you are the one and only fourth patient, so I'm sure you can figure all of this out. It's not like it's rocket science. Okay, maybe *it is* rocket science, but rocket science can be overrated. At least, that's my humble opinion."

"Thanks doc. I didn't know you had a humble opinion. In any case, let's finish up so that I can head back over to Mission Control. I think the answers are waiting for me there."

"Great! We'll take everything your insurance is willing to pay and you can see Sarah on your way out for your next appointment."

Chapter 3

Emptiness

It was expected that the arrival on Mars would have a record number of viewers on earth. Of course, because of the distance from earth, a live broadcast of the first steps on Mars, or anything else the crew might want to send, would be delayed by fifteen minutes or perhaps more. So, it had been decided long before their arrival on Mars that important events would be recorded for playback later on earth, which would also allow them time to edit their broadcast to provide the best possible impression to their viewers. Cameras and rovers had also been strategically placed to pick up much of their activity while on the red planet. Housing, food, water and other essentials had been sent ahead of time and would be available for use during the planned three-month mission. That three months would also allow the planets to be properly positioned for a shorter trip back home, so it was important for everything to happen according to schedule.

Although they had landed safely, because they had to do so manually, they did not land exactly at the planned location, so some important footage may not have been captured. However, they were going to use whatever video equipment they had to make sure there was a record of their arrival. They got into their spacesuits, eager to make those first steps on the surface of the red planet. They could still speak to each other through the amplifiers in their suits and be picked up by the recording equipment as they left the ship, so their words could be replayed for years to come.

Captain Dave opened the exit door on the side of the ship by turning the heavy metal handle a 90 degree turn counterclockwise and rolled out the chain link steps from there leading down to the surface. He looked down below, just to view the Martian surface for the first time close up. He thought it looked rather rusty, even though there was no water to create rust. Perhaps metallic was a better way to describe it. He wondered how the first step on the surface would feel, whether it would be spongy, solid, or just plain dry. There were 12 steps from the exit door leading down to the ground, and they had to carefully maneuver their hands and feet one step at a time as they worked their way down. After being weightless in space for seven months, they noticed the pull of gravity on their bodies, although just over a third of the weight they would be on earth. Still, it was a sudden change after feeling weightless for so long and would take some getting used to. It was early in the Martian day, and the temperature was a seasonal 57 degrees below zero Fahrenheit. Fortunately, their spacesuits protected them against such extremes in temperature. Brandy tugged on her dad's spacesuit to make sure he was paying attention.

"Dad! What are you going to say when you step on Mars?"

"I'm thinking about it."

"Just *now* you're thinking about it? You have to get it just right, because whatever you say will be in the history books forever."

"I've got it!" said Kristy. "Say 'In the name of the Whitney family I claim this planet as our home forever!'"

"I don't think I can say that."

"Sure, you can dad, just repeat after me."

"No, I don't believe I'm authorized to claim the entire planet for us. There are things like international treaties that forbid it. Besides, there's probably some parts we don't want."

"You mean like when Russia didn't appreciate Siberia enough, and then it started thawing and exposing more history?" said Kristy, "and then they brought back the woolly mammoths and put them in zoos. Can we go to Russia and see a woolly mammoth when we get home? I've never seen one in person."

"I'm not sure where you're going with that. Besides, by the time we get back there will probably be one at the San Francisco Zoo. Let's just focus on getting to the surface."

They made their way down to what turned out to be a dusty, dry Martian surface. Dave was about to step onto the surface, but Kristy was following too closely behind and bumped her foot into his helmet from above, causing him to lose his footing and trip his way down to the surface, falling and rolling on his side.

"Dad! You hit the surface without saying anything historical."

Dave first muttered a few expletives under his breath he was sure no one heard before he spoke up clearly. "All I can say is that I've landed. Now help me up."

"Okay, but that won't look good in the history books. I can edit it for you later to say whatever we want, and no one will be the wiser. Once it goes viral, everyone will believe it." The rest of the family followed down the swaying chain link stairs carefully until all were standing on the Martian surface, quite satisfied at having achieved this amazing milestone. There was a moment of silence while they just took it all in, and caught their breath. They kicked around some dust to see what it would do, noticing that it stayed suspended above the ground longer than they expected. They had viewed countless videos of the Martian surface, but now for the first time they were immersed in the Martian environment. The surface was dustier than they imagined, but they could understand why this was called the red planet. This dull red rusty looking dust covered the surface, even though below the dust it was quite rocky. Depending on where they stepped, perhaps their footprints would be visible for some time.

What might a deeper analysis of the Martian soil reveal about the history of Mars? Might they uncover things that will prove valuable on earth later?

No doubt they would bring many samples of dust and rock back to earth later with them. They wondered if there would be any sharp rocks they would have to be careful to avoid. They had been assured that their suits were triple puncture resistant, although no one actually explained to them what that meant. It would later be revealed that someone at Mission Control came up with that term to give them more confidence in the success of the mission, and if later pressed for an explanation, they would come up with the three things covered by the term *triple*. As they looked out over the landscape it appeared there were just light winds, though of course those winds lacked the oxygen necessary to sustain them. Dave recalled that day back in 2021 when the first recorded sounds from Mars were sent back to earth. He switched on the external microphone on his suit to hear Martian sounds for the first time live, and the rest of his family did the same. Of course, they would have to keep their suits on until they could reach their habitat, which once in place would then be sealed from the outside and be able to hold breathable air, a mix of nitrogen, argon, and oxygen, while also maintaining a comfortable temperature.

"Dave, can you get a reading on where we are in relation to our new home?" asked Kate. Kate was more focused on the way things looked than evaluating their instruments and looked to her husband to decipher that information.

Dave could read the data showing up in his helmet camera to see their relative position in comparison to the established coordinates for the supplies that had been sent ahead. Since they hadn't worked out a very tight coordinate system for Mars yet, the numbers he would get would be a rough estimate, sort of like when your GPS tells you that you are traveling on the raised freeway when you are really on a surface street, or maybe when it takes you off the edge of an old bridge no longer in service, a mistake you are unlikely to make twice. "It looks to be about a half mile walk to the calculated coordinates, just over that hill," Dave said as he pointed ahead. "Then we can inflate our home and enter." Their suits also had built-in water packs to keep them hydrated when they had to wear them for any length of time.

"It will be just like camping," said Brandy, "without the bugs." At least, Brandy *hoped* there would be no bugs. She asked her mom one day some years ago what they would do if they got to Mars and there were bugs everywhere, and Raid didn't work on them. How does a mom answer such a question? Brandy was young enough that all she had to say was, "Of course it will work honey! You've seen their commercials. And daddy will step on the rest of them." Of course, as Brandy got older, her mom could assure her for multiple reasons that they would not have to fear any bugs on Mars. Still, Brandy slipped a can of Raid onto the spaceship just in case. She never thought that the lack of atmosphere in space would result in the pressure inside the can pushing out, causing it to explode. Fortunately, it was packed tightly away when that happened a few miles above earth and no one was hurt.

"I'll race you there," said Kristy, as she took off running in the assumed direction of their new home. Brandy just stood there and looked on, shaking her head and thinking she would catch up later anyway. She couldn't quite figure out how Kristy adjusted to the gravity so quickly after seven months in space. She just added that to the list of things she didn't understand about her sister. She figured that Kristy's enthusiasm would help test the limits of what was possible on Mars, whether it was running a half mile in a bulky spacesuit or seeing how much space macaroni and cheese you could eat without taking a second breath.

"You realize all of this is being documented, so people will be watching these events for a long time," said Kate. "You already tripped your father once."

"There goes our privacy," said Kristy, as she paused to look back since no one was taking up her challenge. With the equipment in their suits they could actually hear each other's conversations from about five miles away, much like walkie talkies. Mission Control determined that to be a sufficient distance to keep them all connected verbally. They continued on their way, feeling surprisingly comfortable given the outdoor conditions. The spacesuits worked just as they were designed, providing safety in a harsh environment. They had a lot of practice using these suits on earth as part of their training. That was under the full gravity of the earth, of course, but it still got them used to the bulkiness of them. They knew that once on Mars they would spend a lot of time in them. So, they adjusted well to using them on Mars and approached the top of the hill in about 20 minutes, eager to see everything laid out for them on the other side, although lagging behind Kristy. Kristy had charged on ahead, deciding now it was a race once again. She told them, "I feel great. What gravity?" She got to the top of the hill well ahead of the rest and then came to a sudden stop, as she stared across down the hill, speechless. As the others made their way up the hill toward her they expected some reaction from her before they got there. She may have been expecting her dad to say something like: "Cat got your tongue?" She continued to just stand there until they caught up with her. They walked up behind her to share the view. Much to their surprise and shock, they peered over the hill only to see nothing but an empty, barren landscape.

"Where's our home?" asked Brandy. "Where's all the supplies?"

"Mars rats!" said Kristy, still maintaining her sense of humor that she was determined to make a memorable part of their trip and of the reality show of their life here. "They ate all of our stuff! I will be filing a complaint with Mission Control."

"Dave, are you sure this is the right place?" asked Kate. "It *is* a large planet. We could be anywhere." Sure, *now* it's a large planet. All we heard for years is that it was ten times less than the mass of the earth. That explained why it couldn't hold on to its atmosphere. There was a lot of talk about terraforming Mars, but realistically there would be only so much that could be done, given the reduced mass compared to earth and the longer distance from the sun. In any case, Joe Schmoe wanted to make the most of what Mars had to offer, using this mission as a step toward that end. Surely they would find a way to achieve their goals.

"I'm *positive* we're in the right place. This matches the coordinates and the appearance of the expected location. Trust me. I know what I'm doing. That's why I get paid the big bucks." One thing about Dave was that he *always* knew what he was doing, even when he didn't. Kate was his ideal complement, if there was such a thing. She would know when to have him check himself to be sure he *was* doing the right thing. That made them both right for this mission.

Kristy also brought along shampoo and other items she was sponsoring to advertise while on Mars. She was always looking for opportunities to slip in an advertisement, as she got paid each time she did one, as stated in her contract. "I think everything on this planet looks the same," said Kristy. "We might be in the wrong place. But even when I'm in the wrong place I still use Kristy Shine toothpaste and teeth whitener." Kristy held up a tube of toothpaste and smiled.

"Bad time for a commercial shot," said Brandy.

"Cha-Ching!" said Kristy.

"We're in the right place," said Dave. "I'm sure of it. Bring up the images on your helmet cam and you'll see this location matches the shape of the terrain and horizon exactly. We have pictures that were taken by the nearby rovers." Each helmet had the same map and tracking technology. Kate, Kristy and Brandy all got the same readings, which confirmed their location.

"Well, the micro-computer does verify a 100% match for our view and the database," said Kate. "But we *know* the habitats arrived here. The rovers and cameras confirmed it. We even saw pictures of it. Come to think of it, where *are* those rovers? How far could they have traveled?" They began to scan the surface in all directions to locate any rovers. From the latest information they had, surely they would be able to spot at least one of the rovers. Yet they did a diligent search and found nothing, not even the tracks of the rovers.

"We are going to have to return to the ship," said Dave. "We can contact Mission Control from there for further direction, even though I hate asking for directions. Perhaps there will be a message there waiting for us. They must have figured out our location by now as well."

"After that long walk, we have to go back another half mile?" said Brandy, clearly objecting but realizing they had no choice. It was the only shelter available. Her sister reminded her this was just a Martian half mile, not an earth half mile. Brandy wanted to punch her through her suit. They turned around and began the journey back to the lander. This gave Brandy some time to reflect on their journey that had taken them this far. She was only eight years old when they started competing with thousands of other families and groups for the chance to be selected for this amazing experience. Of course, chance had little to do with it. There were rigorous tests, hundreds of hours of classroom study and real-life simulations. She and Kristy were questioned, interrogated and questioned some more to make sure they *really* wanted to do this. At the academy, the instructors and scientists did their best to try to scare her and her sister away from space travel. They had seen many others come to tears and be removed from the course, really for their own good. The academy had to be sure that they were ready for the real thing. Brandy and Kristy held it together, along with their parents. They really wanted this. When they found out five years ago that they had been selected, they couldn't have been happier, but they knew they still had a long way to go. Brandy thought about how this was going to change her whole life. They were already famous from the time they were selected, so that would bring its own challenges long before this trip. And now they were here. They had come so far. She still couldn't believe that this was real, that they had made it.

On the walk back, Kristy was reliving their trip from earth in her mind. There were all those comparisons of this trip to the moon landings, but she knew this would be far different. It was okay for the first couple of weeks of their flight from earth when they could still have normal conversations with friends on earth and with Mission Control, a room full of people cheering them on every step of the way. By the third week into the trip there was about a minute delay between anything they would say and its reaching its recipient on earth. Conversations took longer with more extensive pauses in between. After three months of travel it took at least five minutes for each message to reach its destination. It would get quieter and lonelier as they found that soon they could mainly communicate just with each other, but at least they had each other. They also had the same challenges to keep using their muscles in zero gravity as they would inevitably lose bone and muscle mass over such a long period in space.

After a long half mile walk across the Martian surface, they finally arrived back at the lander. They looked back up at those stairs they had descended just over an hour ago. They did one last perimeter check before climbing the steps and getting back aboard. As Dave got to the top step before opening the door to climb aboard, he took one more look from his elevated position. He knew what his instruments told him. He knew they were on Mars. It just felt like they were somewhere else, which of course they couldn't have been. "Dave, it's okay," said Kate. "Let's get aboard." Dave opened the door and the family all got on board. Dave shut the exterior door and then they entered the main room of the lander.

Dave was doing a lot of thinking too and just couldn't figure it out. *What could have gone wrong? We just sent a message to Mission Control on our way to land well over an hour ago, yet we have heard nothing since. Usually we get at least an acknowledgement.* He sat down at his mobile workstation and began working on a message to update Mission Control on their current status, hoping for some direction or at least confirmation that the world knew that they were there.

Kate couldn't help but think about the many times she would second guess herself about this whole trip. *What were we thinking, taking our children into space?* They were so young when we started to plan this. There was so much at stake, so much that could go wrong. Then she would bring herself back down to earth, figuratively speaking of course, realizing this was a once in a lifetime opportunity that they would never forget. *Everything in life has its roadblocks and obstacles, but we get through them. We'll get through this as well.*

Dave continued to edit his message, realizing all of mankind might end up reading it one day. One message could reveal exactly the type of person he was, so he had better make it a good one.

But what about Joe Schmoe? He promised they would find a way to shorten the trip to Mars. He was going to get it down to 30 days. That's what everyone believed before they were even chosen for this mission. As the Mission Control staff worked hard to fulfill that goal, they discovered along the way that many of their assumptions were wrong. Their testing and experiments did not reap the desired results. The money in their budget began to run low. Then somehow, they ran out of time. They just had to get into space and to Mars first, regardless of the length of the trip. So, it would still be a long trip to Mars, one of the things they agreed to in the fine print should it remain the *most viable* option. There were hundreds of pages of *fine print.* What else might they have missed in the *fine print? Or maybe it was hidden in the language of those agreements they had to accept with every update to the Mission Control app.*

Dave sent the message to Mission Control: "We have arrived safely on Mars. Our equipment confirmed our location. No sign of our supplies or rovers. Please advise." Hopefully, Mission Control could figure out how far they were from the planned landing site. Still, they reviewed their maps and checked their data regarding their location, and it all suggested that they were where they believed themselves to be and that they had walked to the site where their living area and supplies had been sent. They were the first people on Mars. Everyone should know that. How could they not know that? Minutes turned into hours with no response from Mission Control. There was nothing wrong with their equipment, as far as they could tell. All indications were that their messages were being sent and that they had the ability to receive messages. If only someone were listening. It wasn't like Dave could just open up a window and yell at someone on earth from this distance to get their attention. They wondered if somehow something, or someone, could be interfering with their signals.

They realized that if they couldn't locate the supplies that were sent ahead, they would have no choice but to return to earth. Just reaching Mars and walking on the surface was a major accomplishment, yet how much more they could have learned in a three month stay here. Of course, back in orbit they would still have everything needed on their ship to get home, although the journey would be longer given earth's current location. They would just have to ration out their food to make it last for a longer journey. Making their fuel supply last would be another issue.

As the day reached its end and they had received nothing further from Mission Control, they determined that it would best to blast off and head back toward earth. The frustration clearly showed on their faces. After so much planning and through no fault of their own, (yes, of course, no fault of their own) they were compelled to cut their trip short. No doubt they would be able to make contact during their return trip and get some answers. They were able to communicate in space all the way here, so once out in space again everything would be fine. So they all strapped themselves in and went through their launch checklist. Dave fired up the rockets and they successfully lifted off the surface. As they gained altitude, Dave picked up the signal from their ship in orbit and headed toward it. He had to do some quick calculations since they took off at a time when the ship was at a different location in its orbit. He moved toward it and had to do some manual thrusting to get in position. As he approached it he didn't line up perfectly and bumped into the attachment on the ship. He backed off a bit and lined up for another try. This time he made a good connection and they linked up successfully and headed away from Mars. As they said goodbye to the red planet, again they approached that unusual cloud or fog. They still didn't understand what it was, but they had passed through it the first time with no ill effects, so they continued on ahead, passing through it once again in order to leave orbit.

Chapter 4

Ratings

Back on Earth, Joe had finished up with the doctor, receiving a good bill of health, hopefully covered by insurance, and left his office. He headed straight to Mission Control. Mission Control was further south down the peninsula, about a half hour drive without traffic, like that was ever going to happen. The world in general considered San Francisco to be the home of Mission Control, much like they viewed it the home of the 49ers. Both actually were in Santa Clara, but most people had no idea where that was, so for convenience San Francisco was broadcast as the home of Mission Control and future home of the capital of the Federation of Planets, if there ever would be such a thing. Still, Joe had to regularly make this drive down the peninsula. You would think that with his job title he could own one of those mansions with its own helicopter pad between here and the coast, allowing him to fly right over the traffic, but that was not to be.

Putting all things in perspective, that's nothing. Reflecting back, it was a logistical nightmare fighting for airspace on the day of the launch, being so close to the airport. Hundreds of flights were changed to other Bay Area airports, which conflicted with other flights at those airports. It didn't matter because the most important aircraft to get in the air on that day seven months ago was the spaceship to Mars. The whole world followed all the events leading up to the launch. Everyone remembers exactly where they were at the time of the blastoff.

Each member of the first family to Mars had been interviewed numerous times in the weeks leading up to the launch.

Interviewer: "What are you going to miss most about earth?"

Dave: My steak dinner with a cold one.

Kate: The scenery.

Brandy: Boys.

Kristy: Air. No, wait! Oxygen. I don't really care about the nitrogen and carbon dioxide. Of course, without the nitrogen the oxygen would be highly flammable, so I'll say air, unless of course there *is* nitrogen on Mars, in which case I change my answer back to oxygen. Oh? No nitrogen on Mars? Okay, I'll go with air.

Interviewer: "What is your greatest fear?"

Dave: I have no fear, but if you need an answer, it's that we don't make it back, and I'm not afraid that will happen. Call me Admiral. I'm not afraid I won't make Admiral, so let's take that off the table right now.

Kate: That this doesn't go as planned and my daughters never speak to me again. I hope I didn't make promises I can't keep.

Brandy: Boys. Wait, what was the question?

Kristy: When they take the first picture of us on Mars, and my eyes are closed in the picture. I always open them too soon, and then they dry out because I'm afraid to blink again. I hear the air is really dry on Mars. Oh, that's right, no air. Could they just take video instead and pull out a good frame to use? Why is the budget so tight?

Interviewer: "What message do you have for the world?"

Dave: Push your limits. Get out of your comfort zone. Ask yourself, "How hard can it be?" Then go there. Be Captain Dave. Fill my Captain shoes once I become Admiral Dave.

Kate: Cherish every moment you have, and the people you love.

Brandy: Stay out of my comfort zone.

Kristy: Find your own planet. This one's ours. But when you do go there, be sure to take along an ample supply of Kristy Shine Hair Conditioner, because you're going to need it.

All of that was in the past now as Joe made his way through traffic. Joe's drive today took 45 minutes due to traffic, which was not at all surprising. The drive had actually improved in recent years as autonomous cars began to dominate the roads, leading to less drivers cutting each other off and improving flow. He arrived at Mission Control and headed straight inside to speak with his Operations Officer Steve, as reporters gathered outside looking for any breaking news. "Steve, do you have anything more for me? That crowd outside is becoming more unfriendly by the minute."

"Sorry, Joe. Still no word from the crew, now 16 hours from our last communication. Total radio silence."

Joe fiddled through a stack of papers on his desk, which had been there for at least seven months, as if that would tell him something. He looked up at the high-definition monitors on the wall that stretched across the control room. It displayed feed from rovers, drones, satellites, and cameras. This was far more than the early moon missions had. Nevertheless, all was still. "We know the path they were on. I want you to focus any cameras we have on their flight path to Mars and start reviewing existing footage for anything we might have missed. Also, focus my time-space displacement locating device in that area."

Steve looked back at Joe in frustration. "You mean the one with the telescope orbiting earth? You realize that's like looking for a needle in a haystack."

"Yeah, I get that a lot."

"Given its distance from Mars, I wouldn't expect to get any clear information from it."

"Well, give it your best shot." Joe had a lot of faith in Steve's best shot.

Just then Dan, who works with the media to keep the public's interest in the mission alive at any cost, came barging in with his hair in a mess and carrying a messy stack of papers, as usual. "Joe, I need something to keep the story going. You have to contact the crew. If people start to believe they're dead, then we're dead. We lose our ratings and our funding. We're approved for a hundred more missions, I mean episodes."

"Well, I'd sure hate to see you miss a paycheck Dan," said Joe sarcastically, adding, "And I am so glad to hear your concern for our astronauts that are putting their lives on the line so you can have a TV show.”

“You know I care,” said Dan. “or we wouldn’t have gotten *this far*. Without this show, your funding will dry up faster than a snowman in Death Valley. So, it’s not just *my* TV show. We’re all in this together, so just get some answers.”

“We’ll figure it out Dan,” said Steve. “After all, we’re the smart ones. Could I reuse your Death Valley illustration, maybe with something that makes sense?” Dan walked out of the room, not really listening to anything that was said after his last statement. He wasn’t interested in their trash talk. Joe looked off into the distance, which would be the far wall of the room, thinking for a minute, as they continued to receive silent video from the rovers, with no sign of life. They could see the habitat area, still untouched.

“You’re right Steve. We *are* the smart ones. They are out there. We just have to find them while we still have time.”

Chapter 5

U-Turn

Mission Control
Two days after the landing

Joe got called back to Mission Control on an urgent message. He realized that to get inside he was going to have to get past the mob of press that had gathered between him and the main entrance. He grabbed his hat and held it in front of his face as he walked, but it didn't take long before he was recognized. Then the barrage of questions began. "What can you tell us about the first family on Mars?" "What are you hiding?" "Did they die in a fiery crash?" "What are you doing to find them?" "Was it irresponsible to go to Mars?"

Joe said something like, "We're doing everything we can and will have answers for you soon," as he kept walking through the crowd and into the main entrance. He walked into the area restricted from the press and entered the main command room where he was met by his Operations Officer Steve.

"Joe, I did what you said and focused my attention on any footage we've picked up on our satellites orbiting Mars and found something I can't explain. Maybe you can. Have a look."

Joe took a seat in front of the monitor and watched as the footage was played. He observed the spaceship seemingly appearing out of nowhere, traveling above the Martian atmosphere and heading *away* from Mars. Then it made a turn back around toward the planet, closing in and then disappearing, not out of range of the camera, but vanishing, close to where it originally appeared. Joe threw himself back on his chair and almost fell backwards off the chair when he saw this. He wondered if the video just may have stopped recording and then continued, making it appear the ship had disappeared, but something inside of him told him otherwise. "Joe, this was footage from about 15 hours after our last communication, *after* the spaceship should have landed on Mars. After I discovered this, I sent another message to the crew, but still with no response. I checked our surface cameras and rovers and they have still failed to pick up any activity."

"So they never landed? They couldn't have been in orbit all this time. And if they were, they still should have received our messages."

"There's something else. I zoomed in on the area where they vanished. There should be nothing there in that area above the atmosphere, but there is clearly a distortion in our images I can't explain."

Joe looked on in shock as his memories flashed back to Dr. Gonzalez' office. "I think I can. I saw something like this before. About fifteen years before. It just doesn't make sense that it is turning up *here.* Pull up the records on the device on our satellite scanning for time-space displacements."

"You really need to come up with a better name for that device that isn't so long. Maybe an acronym."

"Okay. I'll add it to my bucket list. Did I ever tell you my wormhole story?"

"If you did I don't remember the punchline," said Steve, as he pulled up the data Joe requested.

"About fifteen years ago I went to visit my doctor and ended up going through a wormhole that took me back to Hiroshima in 1945. The blast from the atomic bomb sent me back through the wormhole and I barely got out alive."

"And he's still your doctor? He must be a really good doctor."

"He's the best doctor I'll ever meet. Wait! I'm not really sure why I said that."

Focusing back on the data he pulled up, Steve said: "Okay, so what does this tell you? It appears to be picking up something that shows up in the same area where they disappeared."

"It may explain why they disappeared and are not seen on the surface. They are somewhere else in space or time."

"But Joe, besides the fact that your idea would be like *impossible,* why were they looking like they were going *away* from Mars? It's like they landed and took off again. But we have no footage of them on the surface and no messages from them."

"Think about it. We lost contact with them just before they would have landed on Mars, when they were in this same area. Did they go to a different time and place, like I did? Then they showed up again 15 hours later, traveling away from Mars, and then turned around as if to land, and disappeared in the same area. And now again we can't reach them. But it tells me they may still be in one place, and in one piece. I just don't know if there is a way to contact them."

"Okay, so just for argument's sake, let's say there *is* something to your wormhole theory. What do we tell Dan when he comes looking for an update? They have been missing now for two days. We'll have to tell him something soon."

Joe looked back at Steve. "We tell him nothing! Let's keep this between us until we figure it out. Keep searching through whatever video we have for clues."

Steve thought that was a good idea, primarily because he didn't want everyone thinking that he and Joe had lost their minds. "I'll do my best, but you have to remember our rovers and satellites are only able to see so much. It depends on what is in their line of sight. We just don't have continuous video everywhere we may want to look. I was fortunate to find that video."

"I understand. Anything that you can find would be helpful." Steve returned to his work while Joe stared at the monitors providing the video feed from Mars for anything that might answer their questions.

Chapter 6

Deja Vu

The crew awoke from sleep, unaware of how long they had been out. Captain Dave, sitting in the captain's chair, turned to his wife Kate in the first mate's chair, "For some reason I was going to ask you if you had a headache, but then I realized *I* have a pounding headache. Does that mean something has changed? Are we still on autopilot?"

Kate turned to Dave with a confused look. "I just feel like I have jet lag. Oh, that's right. We're in space. That explains it. We *always* have jet lag." She looked ahead and checked the control panel. "Yes, we're on autopilot all right, but something is wrong. We're heading *away* from Mars. We're on the edge of the Martian atmosphere. How could we have slept through that?"

"Whatever happened, the only way to land on Mars now is to switch to manual, just like they taught us at the academy."

"But Dave, you barely passed that simulation, and that was graded on a curve."

"Doesn't matter. I've got this because *I am the man*. Now I totally understand why they made us go through that training." Dave took a deep breath, not expecting to be in this situation, yet still wanting to maintain Kate's confidence in him, which clearly was in question, even though they had already been through so much together. "Switching to manual."

About this time their teenage girls were aware something was out of the ordinary and came to see what all the commotion was about. You see, even in space, each person spent most of her time in her own room, keeping herself entertained.

"Dad, what are you doing?" asked Kristy. "You don't play video games. You had better let me land it."

"Trust me. I've got this," said Dave as he held the controls and steered the ship around back in the direction needed to enter the Martian atmosphere. "We are right on target now. An Admiral couldn't have done it any better. Am I right, Kate?" A warning alarm sounded.

"Could we disable that alarm?" asked Brandy. "It's *always* going off, and it's *really* annoying."

"Sorry kid," said Dave. "That would defeat the whole purpose of having it."

"It's like the boy who cried wolf," said Kristy. "I know that's an ancient story. I think I learned it in history class."

"Well, this might be the real wolf," said Dave. "And I'm not about to get eaten."

"I don't think the boy got eaten," said Kristy. "I think he got struck down by a lightsaber, an ancient weapon. But I do tend to get my stories mixed up."

"There seems to be some sort of cloud ahead," said Kate. "The computer advises we use caution. Should we send a message to Mission Control?"

"Kate, being this far from earth, Mission Control can only do so much for us. It will take at least 15 minutes for a message to reach them and another 15 minutes after they send us a reply for us to receive it. Besides that, our fuel reserves are quite a bit lower than they calculated for us to have at this point in the journey. How could they have gotten that low? The last time I remember…" he said as he stared off into the distance, as if that helped him to think more deeply, focusing all of his attention in the past. In his mind he thought he faced this same situation before in the simulator. What are the odds that the simulator would present a situation that we would actually face in space? They never get it right. They might as well have aliens firing on us and we get our shields up just in time. Oh, wait! We don't have shields. We could scan for life forms, but we don't have that technology either. "Anyway, if we hold our position and wait for a reply our reserves will get even lower, and we may need them later to get home. I doubt they will see anything that we can't."

"For some reason this feels like deja vu to me," said Kate, "even though I know we just got here. Perhaps we should exercise caution. After all, the computer *is* trying to tell us something."

"Deja vu?" asked Kristy. "Is that the flavor of the month at Baskin Robbins? Are there marshmallows in it?"

"Well, that cloud doesn't appear very threatening to me," said their younger daughter Brandy, ignoring Kristy's remark. "It looks like those cumulus clouds we learned about in school. Just a fair-weather thing. Nothing to fear." Brandy recalled how those friendly cumulus clouds provided the occasional shade the kids needed on a hot day on the playground, or how they used to color them with smiley faces in the first grade, unlike those threatening lightning bolts. She tried really hard to keep her coloring inside the lines. These clouds were our friends.

"My thoughts exactly!" said Dave. "Let's forge on ahead and get to the surface where our comfortable Martian habitats are waiting for us." Dave did it. He set a positive mood and gave the family something to look forward to, even in a harsh environment. He totally understood what it took to make the mission a success. On that note, he then took them through the cloud and they barely noticed the turbulence. They however did notice an unusual rattling sound.

"Hey! That's an unusual rattling sound!" said Kristy.

"Thanks, Miss News Flash," said Brandy sarcastically.

"What could that be, honey?" asked Kate. "That's the first time I've heard a sound like that on our journey. We should note that in the log."

"It seems to be coming from the separation chamber. In any case, we're ready to separate from the rest of the ship to move on to our landing. Hopefully that sound is nothing critical," said Dave. The separation chamber was the last place Dave cared to encounter a problem. He knew it had to function properly for their return trip.

"It just seems odd that after seven months in space now we suddenly have this sound that wasn't there throughout our journey," said Kate. "Something had to trigger it."

"True, but I'm sure we can have a look when we land. Now watch how cool this separation into two parts works." Dave flicked the switch to separate from the larger portion of the ship. At first they were jerked sharply back and forth, and then their ship separated into its two parts, setting the larger portion into orbit around Mars while they continued on toward the surface. However, as he looked back out the viewport, Dave could see debris flying in space between where the two parts of the ship separated.

"Sorry dad," said Kristy. "That wasn't so cool."

"That separation did not go as smoothly as planned," said Dave, "but we are on our way to the surface."

"Will that cause a problem for us on our return, when we have to reconnect?" asked Kate.

"Hopefully those pieces that broke off into space were just extra pieces we didn't need," said Kristy, trying to make light of the situation, which is a great coping strategy for her. "All these ships *do* come with extra pieces, *right?*" she added with a bit of humor and a bit of concern. She sensed no one really had a satisfactory answer and tried to put her concerns out of her mind.

"We can only hope that we will be able to lock back on when it is time to go home," said Dave.

"David Jonathan Whitney," said Kate, "you have to do better than say *only hope* when all our lives are at stake."

There she goes using my full name. "We'll have a look at the condition of our part of the attachment where it connects to the other part of the ship when we land. On a mission like this we expect challenges, and we solve them as we meet them. That's the sort of thing we trained for all these years, and it's gotten us this far."

Everyone tried to recall what training they had actually received to prepare them for this situation. Kate remembered emergency evacuation drills, where they had to suit up and get in the safe portion of the ship and separate from the compromised section before being sucked out into space. She survived about 60% of the time. Brandy remembered several videos they watched, showing the right ways and wrong ways to respond in different unexpected circumstances. "I just remember that most of the people in those videos were toast. That was so it would make an impression on us. I remember all the wrong things to do instead of the right things."

"I do have this certificate showing I was fully trained," said Kristy. "It's even printed in color. Other than that, I've got nothing. So if these colors hold up, I'm good."

"Can you see the landing area?" asked Kate. "We ought to be able to get a reading on that."

"I'm sure we're close," said Dave. "We may have drifted off course a bit, having to switch to manual, so we may have to walk to reach the drop off point where the supplies were delivered for us the last few years. We'll be able to track that location once we're on the surface."

Regardless of the few bumps along the way, nothing could take away from their excitement at this moment when they were about to be the first people to land on Mars. Dave maneuvered the ship into position and safely landed on the planet, just like he did in the simulator 70 percent of the time, or at least 70 percent better than the last guy, who is now stuck at home watching this on television, with no chance of ever becoming an admiral.

They got out their spacesuits, ready to put them on, eager to step foot on the surface. "Girls, be careful with those suits," said Kate. "Why are they so dusty after being in storage for so long? I'm going to have a talk with that Joe Schmoe about this." Once everyone was suited up, they moved into the exit compartment and shut the interior door. Dave opened the exit door on the side of the ship and threw out the roll of steps, letting gravity do the rest as they unrolled down the outside of the ship leading to the surface. After being weightless in space for seven months, they noticed the pull of gravity on their bodies, although just over a third of the weight they would be on earth. Kristy commented that she would have to go back on that diet, even though she was already as thin as a rail. She didn't like that the spacesuit made her look fat.

It was the middle of the Martian day, and the temperature was a seasonal 22 degrees below zero Fahrenheit. Fortunately, their spacesuits protected them against such extremes in temperature. They made their way down to the dusty, dry Martian surface.

"Dad, say something historical," said Kristy. "You're about to step on Martian soil."

"I now step foot on mankind's second planet," said Dave as his right foot landed on the surface, displacing the dust in its path.

"I feel like you should have given that some more thought," said Kristy. "I'm going first next time." They all got their shoes in the soil and observed that there was no breeze to stir anything up, not to mention very little atmosphere.

"Dave, can you get a reading on where we are in relation to our new home?" asked Kate.

"It looks to be less than a half-mile walk to the calculated coordinates, just over that hill. Then we can inflate our home and enter." Brandy mentioned that she wished she had been looking out the portal on the way down so that she could have seen their habitat area from above.

"I'll race you there," said Kristy.

"You realize all of this is being documented, so people will be watching these events for a long time," said Kate.

"There goes our privacy," said Kristy. They continued on their way. It all felt like something out of a dream. Having prepared for several years to take this trip, they all had dreams about what it would be like when they finally arrived. Of course, dreams and reality are two different things. Kristy couldn't help but think about a recurring dream she had for years. They landed on Mars and walked out into the open. Her sister Brandy dared her to pull her helmet off. She thought about it and believed that if she did, her head would explode. Still, not wanting to turn down a dare she said, "I will gladly remove my helmet!" She pulled it off in front of everyone to their horror and nothing happened. She took a breath. "Hey! There was air here all along!" Everyone removed their helmets and thanked her for being so brave. After about five minutes though, when they could no longer feel their extremities and realizing they were freezing cold, they put their helmets back on. That's about when she usually woke up from her dream. She wasn't about to pull a stunt like that in real life, though, unless, of course, Brandy double dared her.

In Brandy's recurring dream, they arrive on Mars to find a community already thriving, producing their own food along with having installed a river and lake, somehow, in the town. Of course, the yards are all landscaped with drought resistant plants. There is real estate for sale for newcomers and growing families already in the community. There's even restaurants and a drive in movie theater. There's a basketball court, because that's a whole different sport on Mars. Of course, everyone drives around in moon buggies. While Brandy enjoyed her dream, she knew the reality would be far more challenging. Yet, Joe always talked about the abundant resources they would discover, and she looked forward to that. They would be like the 49ers, harvesting the Martian equivalent of gold.

As they were nearing their destination, Kristy decided she wanted to be the first to get a look and took off running up the hill. As she was approaching the top of the hill a few minutes later, she looked back to see where everyone was. "Hurry up!" She reached the top and turned to look over the hill. She paused to take it all in. The rest of them made their way up behind her and got their first look.

"Well, what do you think honey?" asked Kate. "Is it everything you expected?"

"It's perfect!" said Dave, as he viewed all of their supplies laid out on the Martian surface. "Let's get over there and get everything set up." They all headed down the hill and got to work inflating their new home and sorting out their supplies. Although there may have been no *ideal* place for their base on Mars, this was considered safer than many locations due to it being in a valley shielded by hills in most directions. Without a protective atmosphere and magnetic field, Mars was exposed to many dangers from space that were out of their control. Still, they had to start somewhere. They had rehearsed this procedure many times before. They called it setting up camp on Mars. Each one knew their role in the set-up process.

Soon their home stood in place, ready to enter. There was an entrance area to the home between the outside and the main living area where they could be sealed in from the outside before going into their home, and it kept most of the dust on the outside. They called it their porch. Since they could remove their spacesuits and walk about freely on the inside after entering the interior door between the porch and main living area, they would want to keep the area as clean as possible from Martian dust and avoid breathing in that dust as much as possible. They brought all their instruments into their home. Kate told Dave where to set everything, and then had him move it all around again, so that it would look "homey". This was certainly an improvement over being weightless in their spaceship for the last seven months.

Now that everything was in order, it was time to prepare a message to send to Mission Control to let them know they had arrived safely. They could do this on the computer station they set up. What an exciting time that would be when the news of their arrival first reached earth.

Chapter 7

Relief

Back at Mission Control, three days after the last contact with the crew, Steve rushed into Joe's office with important news. Joe and Dan were both standing there as he approached. "We just received a message from Mars!" he shouted. Joe ran out of his office, following Steve back to the main command room. Dan trailed behind both of them, making sure he didn't miss anything. The message read: Landed safely on Mars without incident. Took video of the first steps on Mars. We have reached the habitat and are all set up with supplies to sustain us for three months. All are well and in good spirits.

"Well, that's good news," said Joe, "But it still doesn't explain where they were for three days. They don't even indicate anything out of the ordinary. We need to find out what happened."

Dan looked at Joe and then looked at Steve, and then turned back to Joe. "That's not important right now," said Dan, thinking about how he would present this to the public for the most benefit. "They are fine now, and this will be a success story and will likely get us more funding for continued research and development. That delay was just a cliffhanger that helped boost our ratings. People will think we were just stalling for suspense. No one will question it. I can see the headline now: Earth's population, 8.5 billion and Mars' population, 4.

Let's keep the story suspenseful boys, and keep our audience on the edge of their seats."

"We still need to understand what happened," said Joe. "We need to discuss this with the crew. *Something* happened during those three days." Dan even suggested that perhaps Joe and his staff miscalculated how close they were to Mars, and that idea didn't go over very well.

"You worry too much Joe," said Dan. "That will just shorten your life. Let's not trouble them with this right now. Let's make the best of our successful landing. We'll figure out what happened later. There are too many people out there who think this whole trip to Mars is a hoax and I'm going to rub this in their faces. You should too."

"I don't like it," said Joe. "I still want to study all our data and footage from satellites and rovers and see if that turns up anything."

"I'll help you with that, Joe," said Steve. "There's a lot to go through though."

"Then we better get started," said Joe.

"Just be sure you get all their footage about their landing and activity on Mars since," said Dan. "Also, set aside some of the footage and don't let anyone see it for several years. Then we'll reveal it later when it will be worth a fortune. It will be the Mars lost footage tapes. See, I've got this all worked out. You have to think ahead like this. This is going to be amazing. We're making history, boys. In fact, I'm going to formulate a message to congratulate our crew. We'll be showing video of their arrival on Mars for a long time to come. Now let me think of something to say in that message that will get quoted in history books, and make sure they spell my name right." Dan walked out of the room, satisfied with the way the mission was going and mumbling possible quotes under his breath.

"You realize they went *somewhere* these last three days," said Steve. "They must be able to tell us what happened."

"Maybe the answer is not *where* but *when*. The wormhole I went through in Dr. Gonzalez's office fifteen years ago took me back in time. That video we viewed showed their ship disappear and now they are on the surface of Mars three days late. They could have simply went forward in time, and no harm done."

"I'm not sure I want our mission leader believing in wormholes and time travel as plausible explanations. Joe, think about it! Your theory leaves a lot of gaps. Remember, the video we viewed was from 15 hours *after* their initial approach to Mars, and they were at first seen traveling *away* from Mars. What happened between the time of their communication right before they were supposed to land and this video 15 hours later? And then what happened between that video and their arrival over two days later? There are some big gaps here. I think there's more to the story."

"Then we had better get working on a response of our own, because I don't think Dan is interested in finding those answers."

Chapter 8

Move In

It seemed that Mission Control had thought of everything, considering the fact that they received a lot of input, solicited or not, from the family regarding what they expected in their new home on Mars. Brandy made it clear that she wasn't sharing a room with her sister Kristy, or, as she put it, 'the whole deal is off.' Kate just wanted it to at least *look* like a home. She put up several scenic pictures as well as family portraits and decorated with fake plants and flowers because, as she phrased it, 'It's my impression Joe is a little slow in the home making department.' Joe wasn't one to easily take offense, but he *had* lived alone for the past 20 years or so and really didn't give much thought to what a home *should* look like. He didn't have people over to his home much and didn't spend much time there himself either, so it didn't matter much to him what his home looked like. So, he just directed his staff to 'make Kate happy' and stayed out of it. Dave couldn't emphasize enough the importance of a man cave.

What they actually got was a home that was perfectly rounded and highest in the center, with two dividers, one running straight down the middle north to south and the other likewise but from east to west, which made it look a lot like a big tent. They each had a separate room, all being exactly the same size. Then there was a tunnel at the south end that led to a separate main living area where they could all gather as well as take care of their office work. Kate's room was basically her library where she could spend time reading. She had her books all stored on her personal device, and with the special battery from Mission Control not available to the general public, it would hold a charge for ten years, so no electricity would be needed. Dave's room sure was a man cave, with a bar, weights, a pool table and a giant screen television that, you guessed it, got no channels on Mars. Still, he basically had on demand viewing with the huge video library that was provided. Of course, there was nothing to serve at the bar besides your standard astronaut food, although Dave managed to smuggle his secret stash.

"Why do I feel like I'm in one of those bouncy houses?" asked Brandy.

"Sweetie, that's perfectly normal for your first day on Mars," said Kate.

"That's right Brandy," said Kristy. "It says it right here in this self-help book I've been writing for people moving to Mars. I'm surprised I got that one right. I hope the air doesn't smell like body odor after a while. It's not like you can open a window. That's covered in the book too. I'd hate to see future astronauts try that after someone farted or light a match and the whole place blows up because the oxygen level was too high. This book will be a best seller for sure."

"I'm glad to hear Kristy that you are watching out for future astronauts," said Dave. "So now we have to get used to Martian time, but we still have to be aware of earth time, even though our days will be slightly longer."

"It's like having daylight savings time every day," said Brandy. "Bonus time every day, an extra 37 minutes. That might be a selling point to get people to move here."

"So, it's just getting dark Mars time," said Kate. "Of course, daytime isn't exactly that bright either, compared to what we're used to. I won't be wearing my sunglasses."

"I want to get a picture of a Mars sunset and post it online," said Kristy. "At least whenever we have Internet again, that is."

"I suspect Martian WiFi will be along in about a hundred years," said Brandy.

"I like your positivity," said Kristy.

"So what's earth time?" asked Kate. "At least in our old time zone."

"I'll bring up a reading on the computer," said Dave. "It is 7:50 p.m. Pacific Daylight Time. October 24."

"I know we're disoriented as far as time," said Kate, "but that doesn't sound right. Wasn't it October 21 when we were coming in for a landing? Three days didn't pass that quickly. How does this thing keep track of time when it can't access satellites from earth?"

"It's all based on its last readings from earth before we left and keeps running from that time zone, no matter what time zone we're currently in or what our heads tell us," said Dave. "Oh, here comes a message from Mission Control. Looks like our communication is working well."

The message read: That's wonderful news! Your landing is being broadcast around the world. People are buying Team Mars collectibles of all sorts and you are booked for all the late-night talk shows upon your return. Congratulations on your remarkable success! Live long and prosper! Freedom reigns on two planets!

"Well, they don't seem concerned," said Kate. "I suppose we *are* right on schedule."

"That also sounds like someone is trying to get themselves quoted in the history books," said Kristy. "I've prepared a list of memorable quotes I'll slip out gradually over the next three months, so they don't look planned. We'll see who gets quoted the most."

"We will have to investigate the damage to the separation chamber attachment when we have more daylight," said Dave. "In the meantime, let's check out our food supplies, and then we can get some rest."

"Yeah," said Kristy. "Let's make sure the Mars rats didn't get into our stuff."

"What's with the Mars rats, Kristy?" said her annoyed sibling. "That's not even funny! There are no Mars rats. Yeah, you can quote me on that in your silly log."

"What about spiders? You know you're scared of spiders."

"Stop it Kristy!" said Brandy. "You're scared of everything! You just hide it by trying to be funny. One day that's going to backfire."

"Right… But there's a huge cockroach behind you! Made you almost look."

They finally wound down for the night, though it was hard for anyone to fall asleep their first night on Mars. But they all did manage to get some shut eye. They could really sleep and wake up on their own schedule anyway, because what was anyone on earth going to do about it? They would still get paid the contracted amounts in the new worldwide digital currency, straight into their bank account.

Chapter 9

Damage Control

The next day, Dave climbed up on top of the lander to investigate the condition of the attachment. It was clear that it had taken with it a sizable portion of the connections from the main ship. It would need to be adapted to have any chance of attaching to the rest of the ship when going home. The only choice Dave had was to work with the materials on hand. The problem was, he didn't have any materials on hand, except for Mars' *abundant resources,* as they called it. It was assumed that after arriving, they would discover untapped natural resources on Mars. The main reason for believing this was because it would be essential for the continued development of any Mars colony, so of course there would be abundant resources, there would *have* to be. If Earth has abundant resources, then why shouldn't Mars? Yep, just hiding below the surface waiting to be dug up. He was concerned but would avoid showing that to his family in order to keep them from worrying. He realized that with the cameras and rovers present, much of their activity was being recorded and sent back to Mission Control. He also realized they would notice his concern about the lander soon enough, if any camera was picking him up. So, he made it a point to confirm no cameras were looking at the lander before he got on it to check the attachment.

Besides, he could handle this himself and they didn't need to know about it. He would decide what they would see and what they wouldn't. After all, that's why they made him the Captain. He would inform Mission Control about what and when he felt it important to relate.

There was also what they were filming directly that they could store on the computer and send to Mission Control whenever they felt it worthwhile. No doubt people would want to see their first steps on Mars from yesterday, so Dave figured this would be as good of a time as any to send that, so he went back into the habitat and took the data file of what they recorded yesterday from the camera, saved it to the computer, and sent it to Mission Control.

Back at Mission Control several hours later, Steve had received the transmission of the footage Dave sent and was reviewing it, realizing some would be shared with the media, and he would want to edit it accordingly. Joe arrived and viewed the entire video with him, looking for anything out of the ordinary. "Well Steve, It looks like a successful landing. They seem to be adjusting well. If that was a wormhole that took them through time, it appears to have had no ill effects."

"Joe, I know you've been through a wormhole and I haven't, but I just think that if *I* went through a wormhole, there would be ill effects. It just doesn't seem like the most logical explanation. I mean, wormholes don't form every day."

"Yes, of course, but we still need to tell them about the missing three days, no matter what Dan says. We need to find out what *they* know about what happened. I'm going to put together a carefully thought-out message."

"That sounds like a good idea Joe, because knowing Dave, if there was a problem, he would try to fix it himself and not tell us until it is too late. At least I know I can trust you to be completely honest with me. After all, the success of the mission depends on it." As Joe heard the words coming from Steve's mouth while looking toward him, he was careful not to display any hint of the guilt he felt deep inside. After all, he had nothing to feel guilty about.

Chapter 10

Mystery

On Mars, one day later, Dave and Brandy were outside of the habitat in their spacesuits, exploring the surface and scanning for anything valuable they might discover. They also did some digging in the Martian soil to see what they would find below it, but just found more Martian soil, hard, cold and compact. Still, they collected samples they could later analyze. "Dad," said Brandy, "I notice we don't get blue skies here. It's always yellow and brown. Actually, the sky around the sunset looks closer to blue than anything looking up. So, what's up with that?"

"That's because there is so little atmosphere here. When the wind *does* get strong enough to stir up the dust from the surface, it gets up in the sky and stays there a long time before it will eventually settle back down on the surface. That's what affects the color of the sky. There's almost always *some* dust above the surface affecting how we see the sky. But you do have to admit that it is fascinating to be able to walk around and explore and pick up whatever we see. The rovers took much longer to cover any ground, and we can see and touch these things firsthand. We've done more the last couple of days than what the rovers did for decades. You can even pick out your own souvenirs to bring back."

"What about that clause that says everything we find is property of the government?"

"Considering that we're risking our lives coming here, I think there will be some leeway. Just stash some of your find and reveal it over time. Call it your retirement plan."

"I'm glad we came here. Even though I miss home, this is amazing. I hope we make a lot of discoveries. Do you think we'll strike gold?"

"It would be nice to find something as valuable, but at least I'm sure we're going to change the way people view Mars."

Kate came out of the habitat and over to Dave. "Honey, we just got another message from Mission Control. You might want to have a look." Even through their helmets Dave could see the concern in Kate's face as well as hear it in her voice. They all headed back into the habitat to view the message on the computer.

It read: This is Joe. I'm glad to see you are all doing well. We are trying to solve a mystery. You may not realize it, but between the time you sent a message shortly before landing on Mars and when you sent your next message telling us you had landed safely, three days had passed. We have some theories about this, but we need to know what you remember about that time, or anything that would help explain this gap. We feel it would be good to understand this before you leave Mars to return home.

"So the clock on the computer *is* correct," said Kate. "But we lost those three days too. It's like we slept through them, but I know *I* didn't sleep for three days. I sure don't feel *that* well rested."

"We can tell them that we have no memory of those three days," said Dave. "After all, that's the truth, but I'm not sure how that will help them. I find it hard to believe we could have been unconscious all that time."

"What about that cumulus cloud?" said Kristy. "Tell them about that."

"It wasn't a cumulus cloud," said Kate. "But it was quite unusual. Come to think of it, that's where my memory seems a bit cloudy, no pun intended." They put together a message in response to Joe, telling him about the cloud they passed through that seemed to have no affect, but that also they have no memory of those three days.

Chapter 11

Sacrifice

Back at Mission Control, Joe and Steve had been studying the records from satellites and rovers to get any clues they could find to explain this. They found some more footage of the cloud the crew was referring to, but without any clear explanation of what it was. They tried to see if they could analyze its composition, but with minimal results that would provide any answers. They were unable to find any other activity on the surface prior to the crew's landing when they made contact after the three-day gap. What footage they had from satellites did not show any other signs of the ship.

"Joe, maybe what we should be looking at is what would cause them to have no memory of three days. Certain traumatic events could cause short term memory loss. They are in a harsh environment. Perhaps they faced a hostile situation that they cannot recall or that has been blocked from their memory for their own protection. There has to be a logical explanation."

"I agree, Steve. You know, when I went through that wormhole, I didn't lose my memory. I would have remembered that."

"Right. You and your wormhole. So that means it's something else."

"Not necessarily. What if a wormhole is creating a situation that affects their memory? You said it yourself about traumatic events."

"Maybe we should just stick to the facts, to what we know, and go from there."

Joe got to thinking and gave Steve *that look,* the one like a light bulb turned on in his head. "Steve, we have several satellites orbiting Mars right now."

"Yes, we do, Joe."

"So many that most people can't even keep count. So many that if one turned up missing, it wouldn't even be missed."

"Someone in Accounting would probably notice, but where are you going with this, Joe?"

"Let's fly one of the satellites directly into the cloud while another satellite films what happens to it. That could answer some questions."

"You realize that is a tricky procedure to get the satellites just right to film that clearly, but it could be done."

"Then make it so, number one."

"Very well Captain Picard." It took some maneuvering to get everything into position to be able to do that, in fact, it took a couple of weeks just to set it up. By that time it was day 17 on Mars. They really hoped they wouldn't lose their satellite in the cloud, since millions of dollars were invested to get it to Mars, although that is just pocket change in space. Of course, if they *did* lose it, and it was questioned because someone was actually counting satellites, they could just say it stopped functioning, which would be true, and stuff on Mars stops functioning all the time. If expectations are kept low about how long this equipment is supposed to last, the public is happy with whatever use they see come from it. This satellite had been in use for a couple of years, so it had a good run. Right on cue, the satellite flew into the cloud and vanished. They also lost all communication with it.

"Joe, that cloud must have torn it apart. We stopped receiving video from it as soon as it entered the cloud. If it was still in one piece, we would still get a signal."

"No, it's still in one piece. Think about it Steve. The crew went through that cloud and *they* are still in one piece. We just have to find it." Joe paused and stared up at Steve.

"No, you've got that look again, the look like you have a crazy theory that is going to take a lot of my time. Tell me it's not going to take a lot of my time."

"Steve, I want you to go back and search all the pictures from all the rovers we ever had on Mars for any evidence of that satellite we just lost."

"Joe, that would take a lot of my time, and besides, it's gone! What good would that do? Why would I look at old footage from before we sent it through the cloud? And don't say..."

"It may have gone back in time. I know from my own experience that a wormhole can cause that. Thanks to Dr. Gonzalez the radiation poisoning from Hiroshima didn't kill me, so I'm sure this search won't kill you."

"That reasoning of yours is not very reassuring, and that's a lot of footage from a lot of years. Do you realize how long that will take?"

"No, so get started."

Mars Day 6

One of the critical experiments to be performed on Mars by the crew was to attempt to grow food that would actually be edible. An area in the habitat had been reserved for that, and in their first few days the crew set up this area with Martian soil and seeds that were brought with them. Other experiments on Earth and in space to grow food from Martian soil, moon soil and soils considered similar to those had reaped some success, but this would be the first time this would actually be done on Mars itself. Since the Martian soil itself is considered toxic, along with what radiation it may be exposed to, it was unclear if food grown in it here would be safe to eat, so for this trip their food supply was brought from Earth, but this attempt to grow food would help them see what was possible and if it would be edible. They could run tests on the content of anything they might produce. This could benefit future missions.

Another experiment would be to attempt to produce oxygen on Mars. This had been done before, but only on a small scale. Now the goal was to produce something more meaningful. Maybe one day they would be making fuel on Mars as well. These and other experiments would continue to keep them occupied in the days to come.

Mars Day 18

Kristy was out walking with her mom and spotted something unusual on the Martian surface. She walked toward it to get a closer look. She wiped the dust off it. "Mom, this is one of our satellites. It must have fallen out of the sky. I'm sure it wasn't here yesterday.

"Honey, that thing has so much dust on it that it must have been here for years. And look around. None of the ground dust in this area has been disrupted recently. You probably just didn't walk by this spot before."

"Mom, this is the same path I took yesterday. Look! Just ahead of us is where I was digging. And you can see tracks that we left yesterday over there. There's no way I would have missed this yesterday. I'm starting to know this place like the back of my hand, even though I can't see the back of my hand with this spacesuit on."

"This thing could be 30 years old, or older. This doesn't make any sense."

Kristy wiped some more dust off to uncover something else. "No, mom, look at this symbol on the side, the one with two planets on opposite sides of a star in orbit. That's Joe Schmoe's symbol for his company."

"Okay, well it could still possibly be 20 years old. Joe has been around for some time."

"But how long has he been sending satellites here? I'm taking a picture of it to send to Mission

Control. They must have some record of it." Kristy got a picture, which they included in their data transmission they sent later that day.

Mission Control
Day 19

Steve was reviewing their latest data transmission. "Joe, we received a picture from the crew of a satellite that crashed on the surface. Could this be the one we sent through the cloud?"

"Well we have no other record of a satellite crashing that would explain this. But if it just went through the cloud and kept heading for the surface and crashed, we would still have received a signal and video from it up to the crash, but our video feed ended with it entering the cloud."

"Joe, there's something else. If this really just crashed a day ago, it would have stirred up a lot of dust in the vicinity that would have remained suspended for weeks or months, but I see no evidence of that. They also believe by its appearance it has been there for an extended period of time."

"Are we missing any of our satellites?"

"All of our satellites are accounted for, except the one we lost contact with. This must be that satellite. It's location seems reasonable given where we last saw it if it did continue down to the surface. It seems too coincidental to be anything else."

“Okay Steve, so you are keeping count of how many satellites we have. Keep checking the previous footage for any other signs of this satellite. Check any images of this area to see when this first appears.”

Chapter 12

Sky

It was Day 20 on Mars, just after sunset. The family was just outside their home, viewing the nighttime sky. That is one thing they have enjoyed doing regularly since arriving. With absolutely no light pollution, Mars is an ideal place to view so much in the star filled sky, but certain things still stand out. "That's a bright star," said Brandy. "It reminds me of Venus in the Earth sky."

"That's actually Earth," said Dave. "It really is the brightest object in the nighttime Martian sky, at least right now. If you look carefully, you can see the light from the moon near it. That looks like a fairly bright star. It's pretty neat to see both the earth and moon beside each other in the night sky. In a few weeks, we should get a view of Jupiter when *it* will be the largest object in the night sky."

"Well, this proves we really are on Mars and this isn't just some elaborate hoax."

"Of course it's real, even though some people still probably won't believe it when we get back."

"Just to be sure dad, let me try something." Brandy paused. "Computer, End simulation!" Nothing changed as Brandy looked in all directions. "Okay, it's real." With the latest virtual reality technology, it was harder than ever to tell what was real and what was not. It would place you right in the center of the simulation, and it's all generated from an app, so you're not wearing anything bulky to remind you it's not real. It's become really popular with escape rooms.

In addition to the nighttime sky studies, their days also proved to be amazing adventures, whether it was long walks, digging below the surface, or studying the makeup and history of what they uncovered below the surface.

Reports continued to be sent to earth every day, which would add to the knowledge of this place and allow for further analysis by others back at Mission Control and elsewhere. Their broadcasts proved to be the highest viewed shows ever, with even more viewers than the M*A*S*H* finale. They repeated many things that were done on the surface of the moon during the Apollo missions, like to see how far they could hit a golf ball. Dave was determined to break that record in particular. The Apollo records held though, no matter how much Dave worked out. They shared with earth what it was like to live on Mars, day after day, the challenges and the rewards. It was one thing that got others excited about becoming astronauts, along with the new Mars action figures being sold everywhere that included the whole crew. Of course, there were also multiple Mars LEGO sets available.

Chapter 13

History Rewritten

Back at Mission Control on Day 30 of the Mars Mission, Joe walked into the office and he could tell Steve was eagerly waiting to tell him something. Once Steve made eye contact with him, he spoke up. "Joe, you won't believe what I found," said Steve.

"Try me."

"Actually, you probably *will* believe it. I'm looking at it and *I* still don't believe it. The Opportunity rover picked up pictures of our satellite wrecked on the surface of Mars 17 years ago. That was long before we ever sent that satellite to Mars."

"So now we know it really is a wormhole and that our crew may have went on a trip through time during those three days."

"Somehow Joe, I knew you were going to say that. You probably also want to point out that we just changed the past since Opportunity took a picture of our satellite that wasn't built until years after Opportunity stopped functioning. So now I suppose you expect me to believe in time travel."

"Well Steve, it's not like someone has invented a time machine and has been skipping about through history changing our timeline without us even knowing about it. I would never expect you to believe that. But I have experienced how a wormhole can place a person at another time, and I believe that is what has happened with this satellite and it would seem to our astronauts."

"Okay, Joe. I guess that forces me to think outside the box and look at this possibility. I must admit that it appears like you called it. But that doesn't tell us much if they can't remember anything that happened. Could that really affect their memory? Could they get those memories back?"

"Obviously, there are things we don't understand about what happened. We still need to tell them what we found. We may be able to piece together what we know with what they know to figure all of this out."

Chapter 14

Camera

It was now Day 33 of their mission on Mars, as the crew was informed that the cloud they passed through was actually believed to be a wormhole capable of sending them back in time. They were also told about the video of them coming out of the cloud and turning around going back into it and disappearing, and the discovery of that satellite that was found in a picture from 17 years ago, before it was built.

"But we're on Mars in the present right now, not back in time like that satellite," said Kate.

"We did lose three days, so we could have shifted just a little in time," said Dave. "Just count our blessings that we didn't go back decades, before Mission Control could be there to help us, or before our supplies arrived."

"Dad," said Kristy, "I actually had a dream that we landed and there were no supplies for us and we had to leave."

"We've all had crazy thoughts like that," said Dave. "It's all part of venturing into the unknown."

"Then call me crazy," said Kate, "but I've had that same dream."

"Well *I* haven't had that dream," said Brandy. "But I have for some reason gotten confused while awake thinking our supplies were gone."

"What if it's true?" asked Kate.

"What if *what's* true?" asked Dave.

"What if we *really did* land in the past, before our supplies arrived, and had to take off again?"

"I find it hard to believe we landed before and took off and landed again," said Dave.

"Well Dave," said Kate, "just because *you* find it hard to believe doesn't mean it didn't happen. Try harder. I find it hard to believe that satellite went back in time, but what other explanation could there be?"

"That *would* explain our being low on fuel, and perhaps the damage to the connection to the lander from the additional use, though it should hold up better than that. It's probably that recycled plastic they insisted on using from that garbage dump in the ocean. You know the one that they used to say was two times the size of Texas."

The rumor was that the government was finding ways to reuse plastics disposed of in the past before the manufacturing of such plastic was banned by the UN. Of course, much of the so-called garbage dump by now was made up of micro plastic that had sunk to the bottom of the ocean, but because the government seemed to face one financial crisis after another, Dave believed they cut corners wherever they could with inferior materials.

"Well, isn't it still two times the size of Texas?" asked Kate.

Perhaps no one was keeping track anymore. After all, in 2029 they shrunk Texas down to place that neutral zone between Texas and Mexico so that drug traffickers couldn't build a tunnel long enough to get across it, effectively changing the meaning forever of the phrase "two times the size of Texas".

Their girls found it hard to believe that they couldn't remember more of what they may already have done on Mars. If that is what really happened, though, they thought that would make a good plot for a movie and wanted to claim the rights to it. They couldn't understand how going through a wormhole would cause them to lose their memory. They tried to remember what happened before landing on Mars and recalled they had all been asleep and realized they were traveling *away* from Mars but couldn't remember what put them to sleep. They felt like they could remember bits and pieces but weren't sure if that was just their imagination.

"Since we were heading *away* from Mars when we woke up," said Dave, "we may actually have already *been* on Mars and took off, flying into the wormhole as we left the planet. We could have been thrown around, suffering a physical trauma that knocked us unconscious and caused us to lose our recent memory."

"That's not going to work for the movie, dad," said Kristy. "We had to fight this giant space monster, and the only way to get rid of him was to let him take our memories, since he was a very private monster and didn't want us to remember him. But then, the human spirit was so strong that we recovered our memories through sheer will power. Then we went back and blasted that monster."

"Nobody is going to go see that," said Brandy.

"I bet you're the first one in line," said Kristy.

"But we remember traveling through the wormhole when we were going *toward* Mars without any problem," said Kate.

"Perhaps traveling *against* gravity, Dave speculated, "made it more difficult to escape the effects of the wormhole and we experienced something that affected our memories."

"If we really *were* here before," said Kate, "we would have done some of the same things before."

"Like filming our first steps on Mars!" said Brandy.

"The camera!" They realized that while they downloaded video each day from the camera, they never considered what may already have been recorded on there previously. They may have filmed themselves and not transferred that to the computer. A previous visit before taking off again would have had to be brief, since all their supplies were still here when they landed this time. They searched the videos on the camera from the beginning and to their surprise and shock found *three* other occasions of their first steps on Mars still stored there. They all sat back, flabbergasted.

"How could we have landed *three* times?" said Kate. "How could we not *know* that? And how has it affected our mission and chances of getting home?" But then why would they take off without using their supplies? They realized that they could have gone back in time, much like the satellite, to a time before the supplies ever arrived. They may have gone back too far to contact Mission Control as well. So, they would have headed home to earth, only to pass through the wormhole again and lose their memories again, apparently an affect the wormhole and their journey through it was causing each time they left Mars. Back on that side of the wormhole going away from Mars, they must have shifted to a different time again and that was why they were seen on video 15 hours after communication was lost, appearing out of nowhere from one of their previous landings on Mars. But not remembering what happened, they turned around and landed again, making another video upon landing. They finally landed at the right time when their supplies were waiting for them. So now that they thought they knew what they were up against, they had to make sure that when they finally did leave, they would make sure to somehow tell themselves that it was time to return to earth, just in case they lost their memories again. They were proud of themselves for having figured this out on their own and decided to gloat to Mission Control about it.

Chapter 15

Options

The next day back at Mission Control, Joe and Steve brought Dan up to date on what they knew about the wormhole and Dan decided to work it into their TV show, adding to the intrigue *and* their ratings for the remainder of their Mars stay. Of course, since that sounded more like science fiction, it increased doubt among many about whether they were telling the truth about this mission in general. "You expect us to believe that our astronauts are traveling through a wormhole to different points in time? That sounds like more of those made-up stories of Joe Schmoe, the guy they called the fourth patient. He's just trying to promote himself." That, along with the fact that they were adding special effects to the show to make Mars look more exciting, was confusing people about what was real.

While the rest of the world was being entertained, Joe's biggest concern right now was *getting his crew home safely.* "How much fuel have they used up, and do they still have enough to get home?"

"We did have a built-in cushion in case additional fuel was needed," said Steve. "But more fuel is more weight, and we could only take so much. They are cutting in significantly to the fuel they should be using on the way home."

"What are our options, Steve?"

"Perhaps they can use the abundant resources on Mars to make fuel."

Joe had always talked about the abundant resources he believed were on Mars and would help sustain life, but now he was face to face with the reality that this really was a matter of life and death. Would they really be able to find and use those abundant resources? He couldn't help but think back to some of the things Dr. Gonzalez had said to him in their conversations. "You don't actually believe those stories the public is told? The earth is where abundant resources can be found. Mars is out of my comfort zone, missing air, food and water." What if Dr. Gonzalez was right? We can't make fuel on Mars, at least not right now. We had no idea what to expect as far as actual usable resources on Mars. Joe had seen that the mismanagement of earth's resources was a big part of the reason why people wanted to find another earth, another world to call home. He couldn't admit that though. He just believed the resources that were needed were out there. Dr. Gonzalez couldn't help but challenge that reasoning. "But if we couldn't learn how to properly manage what God gave us here, what would we do on another planet?", he would always say. Joe often thought about that, even though most people didn't believe in God anymore. He thought that perhaps that was part of the problem, along with the way they viewed what they already had on earth. People had lost their sense of responsibility for the earth, figuring scientists like Joe would find them another planet soon enough. Was their trust misplaced? The world had changed a lot since his youth. Still, Mars was the closest answer he could find.

"We can do our best to conserve fuel on the way home, but it will take longer to get home and they'll have to ration what they have. It will be tricky even getting them home if we throw the timing off and Earth is at a different location in its orbit. Joe, we had better carefully analyze our paths home, because there aren't many acceptable ones."

"First let's make sure they get off the surface and don't turn back. They have to remember what they are supposed to do. Do you think we can at least manage that?" Joe shouted in frustration.

"Joe, they can just write themselves notes. Problem solved."

"It may not be as easy as that. In the panic of the moment they may react before they read any such note. And they are more inclined to believe *what they know* than what a note says that they don't recall writing. It will have to be something more obvious, to get their attention. If they land again and burn more fuel, they'll never get home. We'll make sure they plan this carefully. Is there anyway we can take control of the ship from here?"

"That won't work because we first have to establish contact with the ship after it comes out of the wormhole, and any command we send will take 15 minutes to get there and execute. We won't have that kind of time before they turn around."

"With that kind of a delay, we can only travel so far in space with any decent communication. I'd like to find a way to beat the science on that. Anyway, thanks Steve for staying on top of this and keep me posted with anything you come up with that can help."

"Sure thing Joe."

Chapter 16

Dust storm

It was now Day 38 on Mars when the Whitneys witnessed something new. Today the wind picked up enough to stir up the dust from the surface and send it skyward, affecting visibility. There was no accurate way to forecast weather on Mars, and there usually wasn't much to forecast. The family was outside using power tools to drill deeper into the Martian soil when the wind picked up seemingly out of nowhere, so they headed back to their home without striking oil, gold or anything significant. The dust would now spread around the planet and take weeks to clear, given that dust would hover in the air long after the wind abated. The crew would have to limit their time outside of the habitat for a while. This affected some of their research, although the storm itself could be studied close up and teach them about the atmosphere on Mars. Fortunately, their habitat successfully stayed relatively dust free as it was well sealed from the outside. It was also a good test for their spacesuits, which also fared well. It was unclear what affect breathing in some of the dust would have. It was suspect in some runny noses and irritated sinuses, but seemingly no long-term effects were seen. It made for interesting television to see what the air looked like each day until it got reasonably clear. It allowed for some more advertising. "When I have a runny nose, even on Mars," said Kristy, "KristyFreeze throat drops knocks it right off the planet." It did keep the temperature slightly colder outside, not that it was ever warm.

Some people got bored watching the show since they thought it looked the same each day, so Dan wanted them to do something to boost ratings. What about those valuable resources Joe promised the crew would find on Mars? That would get people's attention, but we had heard nothing about that. Joe and Steve told Dan they would come up with some ideas to boost ratings, but they mainly just made-up ideas deliberately designed to irritate Dan. But Dan did go for the idea of giving out prizes to those who could correctly answer the most questions about the mission, along with certain details you would only know if you tuned in to watch the show. (People still said *tuned in* even though their televisions required no tuning.)

Chapter 17

Nightmare

It was still dark on Day 47 in their habitat on Mars. Kate leaped up in her bed. She heard screaming. It was Kristy. Kate jumped out of bed and ran as fast as she could to Kristy's room. She had never heard Kristy scream like that before. She got to Kristy and she was just sitting up screaming. Nothing appeared out of the ordinary in the room. It was 0400 hours, Martian time. Kate came to her and just hugged her and held her tight. Kristy finally stopped screaming and just started crying. "What is it Kristy? What is it baby? I'm right here. You're safe. Everything is going to be okay."

Kristy kept crying, and by now the rest of the family had woken up and come to see what was going on. "It's not going to be okay!" said Kristy. "We all die. I saw it! We were all dead!"

Brandy spoke up: "Kristy, you can't die in your dream, or you wouldn't wake up. It's like when you dream you're falling. You always wake up before you hit the ground. Besides, we're all right here, so we didn't die."

"In this dream, we were already dead. I was looking down at all of our dead bodies, frozen on Mars. It's more of our memories coming back. Just like when I dreamed we had no supplies, and then you all confirmed it. We don't make it out of here! We all die!"

"Honey," said Kate, "it's just all the thoughts of what we think *could* happen. It's not real. You can't remember being dead, and you can't see yourself dead. We're still in control of what happens to us. Your father is going to get us all home safe, despite any setbacks. Tell her Dave."

Dave was caught slightly off guard but quickly recovered before anyone could notice. "Yes sweetie, we're going to be all right. We're going to return to earth and tell our story for years to come."

"Dad, I know you're just trying to make me feel better, but I can tell you don't really believe that. There's something you're not telling us. I can always tell when you're not being completely truthful."

"We're going to make it! It's fine. You worried about those loose pieces we lost in space? We're going to be fine!"

"I never mentioned the loose pieces. You did. Should I be worried about them?"

"Baby, please relax," said Kate. "Your father has that all resolved. He fixed it, so you don't need to worry about it. That kind of worry is what's giving you nightmares. Tell her you fixed it, Dave. Tell her."

"Yes, I fixed it. There's nothing to worry about."

"I know you want to believe that," said Kristy. "None of you have had this dream? None of you have thought this?" They look at Kristy, speechless. "This wasn't something from my imagination. What I saw was real. It was a memory."

"We've all had very intense dreams that seem very real," said Kate. "Just look around you. What you see here is real. We're all here. We're all safe. We're all real. We're just not going to let anything like that happen. We're in this together, and we're going to make it. Okay?"

Kate helped wipe Kristy's eyes. "Okay," said Kristy. "But if we die, I'll be the first one to say I told you so." She half smiled back at her mom.

Chapter 18

Confession

Three days later, Dave approached Kate with a serious and somewhat nervous look. "Kate, I have to talk to you about something."

"Dave, what did you do?"

Dave hadn't had much to say all these weeks about the condition of the attachment between their lander and the rest of the ship. "Connecting back to our ship is going to be, well, it's going to be a problem."

"Dave, what are you talking about? You had it all worked out."

"We have nothing that is a good substitute for the pieces we lost. I was able to attach a hook to the lander that may be able to latch on to the ship, but if too much force is placed on it, it will come apart. Also, we have a limited amount of fuel in the lander, so if we don't successfully connect in a short period of time, we will run out of fuel and fall to the surface."

"Well, we still have a month before we leave, so what do we do?"

"I may have to do a spacewalk to get to the door of the ship in orbit to open it manually."

"So you *can* do that, right Dave?"

After a brief pause, Dave responded. "Yes, of course. Don't even worry the kids with it. I just didn't want to surprise you at the last minute."

"Just make sure you're considering all your options, in case there's a problem with option one."

"Actually, this is option four, given the first three didn't work out."

"Then have option five ready to go. I know you'll get us out safely, Dave."

"I'll do whatever it takes. We never really run out of options."

Chapter 19

The Message

Now on Day 56 of the Mars Mission, it was just another day at Mission Control, with the Mars mission rolling along closer to its completion, until Steve got "the message." "Joe, you need to come in here *now*!" Joe was in the middle of a phone interview with a member of the press. It seemed that in general the public had forgotten about the earlier problems in the mission, now being more accepting of how things were going, so it was safer for Joe to travel freely without harassment. More and more people were buying into the idea that making Mars livable was important to the human race. Many had accepted that it was just a natural progression of man's needing more that would lead to a shortage of resources on earth, and that there were limited resources available, and they couldn't be replenished, so they would have to look elsewhere. So, these opportunities with the press helped his cause to get support for his mission. Of course, even to sustain life on Mars, resources would have to be continually brought from earth. It was unclear if a Mars society could ever become independent from earth. That was their hope, yet they knew they had a long way to go for any chance of that actually being realized. Joe always reassured them that resources would be found on Mars that would make that possible. Others argued that the real problem was that earth's resources had been mismanaged and going to another planet with that same mismanagement mentality would fail to get to the root of their problems. Many of those people still hated all that Joe's mission represented.

However, when Steve spoke with that sense of urgency, Joe knew he needed to drop what he was doing immediately and go find out what was going on. So he wrapped up his interview and hurried over to Steve.

"Joe, perhaps you could explain what this message means." Joe saw it was a new message from Mars, like many they had received before. He read the message out loud so he could both see it and hear it, helping him to process it fully in the shortest time possible.

"Just between us guys, so you don't spend a lot of unnecessary money on an investigation, if for some reason we crash and burn when trying to leave Mars, it's the connection between the lander and the ship in orbit that was damaged beyond repair. It was probably defective in the first place and you should blame the manufacturer, unless of course, that happens to be you. Sue that manufacturer for all that he's worth. If we make it, please disregard this message and scratch it from the record and under no circumstances mention this to my kids or you're toast. Remember, I still know where you live." Joe had to stare out into space for several seconds after reading this while he was still processing it and mumbling under his breath.

"Steve, you know that Dave wouldn't even mention this unless they were *really* in trouble.

He would only say this if he believed they weren't coming back. This is his cry for help." Joe started moving papers around on his desk, as if he were looking for something. "Starting now, we're going to figure out a way that they get back on their ship without their lander connecting to their ship in orbit. Options!" He shouted this as if there was a room full of people to respond, but Steve was the only one standing there.

"Joe, there's no other way on that ship. If they can't latch on in orbit, they won't even be able to maintain their position next to the ship in orbit to spacewalk over to it."

Joe got up and walked over to the whiteboard and grabbed a marker. He wrote at the top of the whiteboard the word OPTIONS in all capital letters and underlined it. After looking around at an empty room he looked back at Steve and said, "Okay, let's try this again." Steve looked dumbfounded and before he could gather a thought, Joe spoke up again. "Can we bring the ship in orbit down to the surface and they board it while on Mars and take off?"

"Joe, there's no way to land the whole ship on the surface without the lander. It wasn't built to land. It would be wrecked. Even if we *could* get it to the surface, given its weight, it would use up too much of its remaining fuel just to blast off again. The only way to board it is while it's in orbit."

"So we need a way for it to maintain its relative position to the lander long enough to get the crew aboard the ship to get them home."

"You also realize Joe that without the lander attached, they can't land on earth upon their return."

"Okay, possibly a water landing, as long as they don't sink and drown. I don't want to know what I *can't* do. I want to know what I *can* do."

"Working on it, Joe. I'll get the whole staff involved on what we *can* do to get them home. I'll order pizza and charge it to your account. That will get them brainstorming."

"I want this whiteboard filled with ideas, good ones, so get working on this. Not a word of this is to leak out to the press. We don't want to start a riot here." As Joe was still talking, an old familiar face walked through the door. "Austin?"

"Bro, I heard you were in trouble and needed my help, so I came as fast as I could."

"Well, I've been in trouble for the last two months."

"Exactly! Just like I said, as fast as I could, so here I am. I see you have a whiteboard with the word OPINIONS written on it. I see I showed up just in time because I have plenty of opinions. First, we need to redecorate in here. This place looks like a morgue hit it."

"Wait, wait, wait!" said Steve. "How do you two know each other?"

"It's a rather long story that is better off told another time," said Austin. "The short version is that your buddy Joe here sucked me up into one of his wormholes and we spent some time in 1976. He promised me a job in compensation. At least, that's the way I remember it. I'm kind of retired now however. I told him I could go to

Mars though if somebody called in sick. That happened on the moon mission. Did you guys ever see Apollo 13?"

Steve managed to cut in. "Another wormhole?"

"You been through one too, bro? They're too unpredictable. You can't travel by wormhole. I recommend a teleporter. You just set it to wherever you want to go. Just don't beam yourself into a cement wall. Always keep your safety protocols activated. Safety first, I always say."

"Joe, does your friend ever stop talking?"

"Just put him on your team, Steve. He might surprise you with an incredibly insane idea that just might work."

**Mars
Day 64**

The air was much clearer as Dave inspected their lander once again, making sure that everything was in order to a reasonable degree given that they would be departing in three weeks. The lander seemed to be unaffected by the dust storm and appeared ready whenever they chose to take off. Dave took video of all the damage to the lander so he could have the computer analyze the chances of it being able to reconnect to the ship in orbit. Initial results from the computer had given it a 0.03% chance of success. After performing all the modifications he could to the lander, the computer brought back a chance of success of 4.7%. Of course, the computer didn't have footage of the ship in orbit in order to analyze that, but Dave didn't like those odds, even though he really didn't trust the computer.

After Dave had finally revealed his concern to Mission Control about the lander being able to connect to the ship, he figured they would come up with a potential idea or two, but he hadn't heard anything yet. He figured it must have been Joe trying to get it just right, even though he could never really get it exactly right. No doubt that was a big factor in Joe being chosen to run Mission Control. His determination to get it just right would help ensure the safety and success of the mission. There was no way that such a tendency could ever work against him. That was his strong point, his one really big strong point, and he was proud of it. In any case, Dave was still going with his spacewalk option if he couldn't get the lander to attach to the ship. The crew also found that over the last several weeks they had recovered bits and pieces of their memory but were still missing the full story. They weren't really sure what to believe, and although they had some memories of having been on Mars before, they were sure that the time spent on any other trip was minimal compared to their current stay, or they would have recalled more. Given that they had survived this far and learned a lot, they considered their mission a success. Mission Control was getting more data about Mars than all other trips by probes and rovers combined. Whatever they were being paid for this, the government should consider it to be a bargain. They had landed on another planet and look what they had accomplished!

Chapter 20

Barnstorming

Now on Day 67, the staff at Mission Control had gathered along with new recruit Austin, and Steve brought Joe into their brainstorming room with a filled whiteboard. It really *was* their brainstorming room. The sign on the door read BRAINSTORMING ROOM. (Actually, two days ago Austin taped a piece of paper to the door with the words BARNSTORMING ROOM. When no one was looking, Steve replaced it with his sign that read BRAINSTORMING ROOM.)

"Well Steve, it looks like you have been busy. So how have we progressed in getting our crew home?"

"They can make use of that wrecked satellite. I can send them instructions on how to magnetize a large piece of metal from it, have them attach it to the lander, and then get next to the orbiting ship. We're counting on the magnetic pull being strong enough to hold while they get the door to the ship open."

"Okay, well it's better than what we had. Let's see if we can refine it to improve their odds. It's a good thing we sent them that satellite by mistake through the wormhole."

"Whatever you say Joe."

"What other options did you come up with? Any ideas, Austin?"

"Yes, Joe, actually I have plenty of ideas. I put together some color schemes that would really change the mood in here and get more production out of your workers. And I recommend that you institute Taco Tuesday, which I invented by the way." They looked back at Austin with a blank stare. "Oh, you mean ideas about the mission." He got a few less than enthusiastic nods. "I suggested drawing up blueprints to retrofit my teleporter for space travel and bring everyone home, but I guess the technology is still 20 years out. That's all I've got."

Joe had already zoned out of that discussion and turned to Steve. He pointed to the whiteboard. "Then what's all this?"

"Actually Joe, all the rest of this writing on the whiteboard is our fuzzy math convincing us the plan will work. We feel it is the only viable option."

"So what would you say are our odds for success?"

"My gut says 30%, but it's been wrong before."

"Then keep working on it and go on a diet if you have to." While Steve would keep working on it, basically he would be compelled to go with the plan he had presented to Joe. Austin then returned to retirement since he wasn't offered a ride to Mars.

Chapter 21

Souvenirs

On Day 77 of their stay, before the break of dawn, the Whitneys awoke to a sound like nothing they had heard before on their visit to Mars, or even in their lives. It sounded like hailstones or an ice storm, only far worse, which of course, would make no sense, with no atmosphere that could cause such a storm. It must have come from outside of Mars' atmosphere. Unlike Earth, Mars offered little protection from what space could drop on them. Dave checked the surface cameras, but it was too dark to make out anything. As an emergency precaution they got into their spacesuits, ready to evacuate. If it were to reach their home, it might cause devastating damage that could render the home useless. "What could that be?" said Brandy. "I'm not afraid to admit that I'm scared to death." It sounded like it was getting closer. It was definitely getting louder.

"Just sit tight and hope and pray," said Kate. "There's only so much we can do right now. We've lived here this long with nothing like this happening, so how long could it really last? After all, it's not the end of the world, as far as I can tell." Mission Control was supposed to have verified that they had an all clear as far as space debris during their stay here. It finally began to subside after lasting for about half an hour.

They waited until it had quieted down before going out to investigate, just while it was getting light. Was it another dust storm? There hadn't been any wind. Fortunately, nothing hit their habitat or damaged it, but the sound was still nearby. It then occurred to them that whatever the storm was came from the direction of… their lander! Dave and Kate hurried in that direction to investigate. It still took them fifteen minutes to arrive at the lander in their bulky spacesuits. The lander had been pummeled with a hail of small rocks, receiving several dents.

"How bad is it?" asked Kate. "Will it still get us back to the ship?"

"Despite all this surface damage, it appears to have maintained its integrity. There's still time to make any repairs if we need to. We can only hope it holds up under the pressure of flying through space. At least once we get back inside the main ship we can seal the lander off and won't need to re-enter it." Dave looked out over the landscape to the west. "But it could have been worse, a lot worse." Dave pointed for Kate to look. The further they looked out to the west, the denser the collection was of rocks that had fallen from the sky and accumulated on the surface. There were literally millions of rocks, some as large as golf balls. They couldn't help but reflect on the fact that something like this could never happen on earth. Here there was no safety net. There wasn't even a warning.

"Well if we wanted to bring home some Mars rocks, we have an unlimited supply," said Kate.

"These weren't Mars rocks an hour ago," said Dave. "They were space rocks. What could have caused this? Where did they come from? It goes on for miles. It had to be something large. But whatever it was, it seems to be over, and hopefully we won't see anything like this again during our stay." They documented what they saw and sent video footage back to Mission Control. The Martian atmosphere provided very little filtering to anything falling from space, but what could explain such a large rain of rocks? Was this a common occurrence future astronauts would need to be aware of? It could have been deadly had it hit their habitat.

**Mission Control
Day 78**

There were just the ordinary sounds of beeps, blips, and cries for more coffee coming from the control room, then Steve got the report from Mars of the shower of rocks and relayed the news to Joe. "Mars is much closer to the asteroid belt than earth, but not that close." He paused momentarily. "Are you thinking what I'm thinking?"

"The asteroid we blew up with the missile?" Joe responded. "Raining down on Mars? But we blew that up over two years ago, and that was millions of miles away from Mars."

"Nothing else would explain that volume of matter in that many pieces. Of course, millions of miles is quite a distance, but in space perhaps that isn't so far. I'm trying to determine if the orbit of Mars could have brought it closer to the asteroid's remains and they could have been caught by its gravity."

Joe didn't hesitate to respond. "Maybe that explains it, Steve. We'll tell the press that if we're pressed for an explanation."

"Really? Somehow, I thought you would put up more of a fight, especially since that theory would seem to be a long shot. You usually hate long shots. It feels like we're missing something important. The explosion would likely have scattered the pieces of that asteroid. It would have taken a strong gravitational pull to keep them all together over millions of miles. Still, I should be able to determine if that is a possibility or if we can eliminate that explanation. I'll get back to you tomorrow on that." Steve gave a nod of acknowledgment and returned to whatever it was he was studying prior to this conversation.

Mission Control
Day 79

The control room was relatively quiet today with everyone minding their own business as Steve approached Joe. "Joe, I've concluded that any debris from the asteroid explosion wouldn't have been anywhere near the orbit of Mars. I don't even think that if it had made that much debris it would have all stayed that closely together for such a long period of time. So it must have come from something else. There's just nothing that seems to explain it."

Joe heard Steve's words, but didn't show any evidence of curiosity about other explanations for the cause of that rain of rocks. "Let's just be glad no one was hurt and move on from this. How about our chances of getting our crew home?" It was clear Joe was changing the subject, and it worked. Steve refocused his attention on Joe's current question.

"I sent the crew the information they needed to best utilize that satellite. There's still a lot of uncertainty with it, but Dave is the right man to make it work if anyone could."

"With so many things going wrong, we're fortunate everyone is still alive, including us."

Chapter 22

Preparations

Nearing the end of their stay now on Day 84, Dave followed the instructions he received from Mission Control and was able to magnetize a chunk of metal from the satellite. Somehow, he thought they would have other ideas, but he went with what they said for lack of anything else that looked promising. He tested his new magnet on objects he had, and it provided a strong hold, but it was hard to imagine that it would hold the lander to the ship in orbit. Given the weight of the ship and the forces upon it in comparison to this magnet, it just didn't seem it could be enough. Maybe it would buy them some time. He felt like he needed a further backup plan. He attached it to the lander so that it would be ready for use when they blasted off in a few days. Seeing a well-established plan that he believed in would also give his family a sense of security, something that they would need, even if it was a false sense of security.

Mars
Day 87

They were on their last full day on Mars. It was hard to believe that after all they had experienced that now it was time to go home.

They excitedly talked about what it would be like when they got home.

"What are you looking forward to most when you get back to earth?" asked Kate.

"I'll have a pizza with every topping I can think of, even anchovies," said Kristy.

"It will be easy to find a boyfriend when I get back," said Brandy.

"Someone who wants to be your boyfriend just because you're famous is more interested in himself than you," said Kate.

"But isn't that a perk of being famous?" asked Brandy.

"One of the challenges of being famous is that you have to be able to tell the difference between your true friends and those that just want something from you," said Kate. "Understand that and you would have matured beyond your years."

"What about you, mom?" asked Kristy. "What do you look forward to most?"

"I want to smell the flowers and the ocean breeze. I want to walk outside without having to wear a spacesuit."

"This will be an experience I will always treasure and never forget," said Brandy. "But it does make me appreciate our home on earth so much more."

"I was getting used to not having to share my planet with eight billion people," said Kristy. "It's going to feel crowded to me. I sure hope they stay out of my way."

"Don't worry," said Dave. "There's still plenty of wide-open spaces."

Chapter 23

Disaster

This was it, Day 88. Finally, it was time to leave the surface of Mars and return to their home, return to earth. They sorted out what they were bringing with them and what was remaining on Mars. There were rocks and soil that could receive further study back on Earth, as well as samples they had drilled down deeper to excavate. They were successful in growing some vegetables, though upon testing they were found to contain a level of toxins that made it questionable if eating them would make someone sick. Further study was required, and they would take the results of their research with them. Most of their video footage had already been transmitted back to earth, but they would continue to make recordings and would still have months in space that would add to their story. Dave sent one last message from the habitat to inform Mission Control they were leaving. Their next planned contact would be when they were back on the ship in orbit, heading home. Dave had rigged the lander as best as he could to connect to the ship in orbit. Since it appeared they would be unable to connect to the ship in orbit the way it was attached previously, they would likely be relying on the magnetized chunk of the satellite to hold them in place while they attempted to board it by whatever means possible.

They took one last look at the enclosure they had called home for the last three months. They were leaving it much as they had decorated it. They had plenty of video footage, most of it transmitted back to earth, to remember it by. The girls asked if they would ever return there again. Their dad told them that they still had the rest of their lives and that being the most experienced ones regarding Mars, they would be invaluable on future trips. They all agreed that this was the best vacation ever, but if someone could open up some good restaurants, that would be a nice improvement. Kristy thought perhaps she would open one up in the future.

They sealed up their habitat and started the walk to their lander. The walk was so much more familiar then when they had first arrived. It seemed they were familiar with every dip, every rock, every potential hazard. For the first time, the reality of their actual leaving was leading Dave to think about what was about to happen with his family, the risks of what they were about to do. He was always so sure of himself, but now he questioned everything. They couldn't remain on Mars any longer. Their food supply was depleted. It was time to go home. He knew what he had to do, or at least he thought he knew. If it took a spacewalk, he would get his family onto the ship.

They arrived at the lander. Everything was very still around them. Conditions seemed ideal for takeoff. They made their way up the stairs and Dave opened the door. They all followed in behind him. They would trust him with their lives.

They knew he could get them home. By this time, Dave was getting some memories back that troubled him. He was remembering things that didn't show up in their videos, that just didn't seem to fit with the full picture. What was he missing, and why? It didn't matter. It would all make sense later. For now, it was time to get out of here and get home. They all got strapped in and went through their preflight checklist. They fired up the rocket and lifted off the surface. They sped up through the thin atmosphere on their intercept course. The lack of atmosphere was a factor that had to be considered as it affected the lander's ability to maneuver. They picked up the ship on radar and headed directly for it.

"Dave, our fuel is low," said Kate. "We're not going to have a lot of time here."

"Then we won't *take* a lot of time." Kate could sense Dave's uneasiness about the situation. They got a visual on the ship and closed in on it. "Okay, there it is. I will be attempting first to lock on to the connector to the ship." Dave got as close as he could to try to latch on to the ship. He had hoped the hook he attached to the lander would have something to latch onto. As expected, it was too damaged from the last separation and lost the latching assembly they needed to attach to the lander. They recalled the debris they saw fly off into space three months earlier. If only they had that back. If only they could have a do over. It was too late for that. "Okay, time to make use of that magnet, courtesy of Mission Control." Dave again had to fly on manual and maneuvered their lander alongside the ship where he had attached the magnetized piece of the satellite. It was difficult to hold a relative position alongside the ship while being careful not to damage their lander in the event of ramming into the ship. They had to get close enough to engage the magnet but avoid a collision that could damage the ship.

"Is it working Dave?" asked Kate. "Is the magnet pulling toward it?"

"I can feel it pulling toward it as I steer, but then it gets out of the magnetic field and I have to start the approach again. Okay, easy does it." Dave finally felt it make a connection, only to separate seconds later as the forces of the ship and the lander pulled this way and that. Just then fuel warning lights began to flash. Dave knew they didn't have much time and made another attempt to connect. This time it held, but for how long? "The only way I can do this is a spacewalk to open the hatch on the ship."

"That's crazy dad," said Kristy. "You'll never make it."

"It's our only chance. Once I get it open, you can follow my path in. I'll walk you through it." By now warning messages were flashing everywhere as Dave headed for the exit. He turned to tell his family he loved them. Just in case, he wanted to have one last look at them and said, "I'm sorry."

"It's not your fault, Dave," said Kate. "You didn't know any of this was going to happen." Dave hurried into the exit chamber and opened the exterior door to outer space. Just as he worked his way to the outside of the door, the magnet separated from the ship and their lander swung wildly away from it as Dave held on to the outside of the door for dear life. He wished the hands of his spacesuit had at least a little more friction as he felt his hands slipping toward the edge of the door, rapidly running out of real estate. Kate grabbed the controls and steered back toward the ship. *I can do this,* she thought, scared out of her wits. There was a hard bump into the ship, and she could only hope Dave was still there with them. "Dave, can you hear me?"

Dave struggled to get a word out as he held on to the door that was keeping him from floating out into deep space. "I'm okay."

There's got to be another way. There's no way we can all get to the ship, Kate thought, as she attempted to lock on again. Kristy came up behind her. "Let me do it. I play video games. Mom, go to dad. Get to the ship."

"You're not sacrificing yourself for me! It's supposed to be the other way around."

"Trust me. Just do it." There was no time to argue about it. Kate just headed for the exit. "Nobody tell me I can't operate heavy machinery with my long hair, Brandy."

"You got this, girl," said Brandy. "I'm following mom."

Kristy thought *I don't need a simulator* as she took the controls and got the magnet to connect to the ship. "Yes!" She made a turn to follow the others. But her emotions quickly changed when only a second later the display flashed everywhere: FUEL TANK EMPTY.

The engine shut off and it was suddenly eerily quiet as the two parts of the ship, still connected, drifted together in space. "Mom," said Kristy, "how long did the magnet hold last time?"

They all realized in the silence that they were out of fuel, and time. "Sweetie," said Kate, now in tears, "14.2 seconds." The ship started shaking with turbulence.

"Stay there Kate," said Dave. "I'm coming back in. It's over."

"What?" said Kristy. "You're my dad! You never give up! You don't tell me it's over! You do that spacewalk, and you get to the other part of the ship and you'll get that door open and we'll all follow behind you and we'll make it on the ship and we'll get out of here!"

"I'm sorry sweetie. We need another five minutes that we don't have. We've used up all our chances."

"What does that mean, it's over?" said Brandy. Before she could say another word, the magnet gave way and their lander separated from the ship and began to drift downward, quickly out of reach of the ship. "Okay, I get it," she was forced to acknowledge. Dave climbed back through the door behind the others and shut them back inside.

"I'm sorry. I failed us all," said Dave. "Let's spend our last few minutes together."

Brandy began to tear up but then put her thoughts together to say what she felt she had to say. "Dad, it was amazing! We did what no human has ever done before. We actually *lived* on another planet for three months. We were successful, no matter how this ends. What we accomplished changes everything."

"Yes, we did it," said Kate, "and I am amazed at how brave you are." Their lander began to increase in speed toward the surface. "I am so proud of you."

"They'll never forget us," said Kristy. "We're a part of history now."

"What you have accomplished," said Dave, "will inspire an entire generation."

"Still," said Brandy, "I was really hoping to have that new boyfriend."

"Me too, Brandy," said Kristy. "Me too." Their distance to the surface closed in rapidly. They all held hands and looked out over the horizon one more time before the sudden impact that killed them instantly.

Back on earth, Mission Control realized that something had gone terribly wrong. "It's been too long. They took off from the surface hours ago. Why can't we reach them? What do our cameras show? Our plan must have worked. They should be aboard the ship by now and on their way home." Joe had sent a number of messages to them, hoping for a response.

"We're no longer picking up any trace of their ship. They're gone, Joe. There's nothing more we can do." It just seemed the mission had been doomed from the start. But who could have anticipated that they would be flung through time? Their fears and assumptions would be later confirmed when they were able to locate footage of the wreckage on the surface from one of their cameras.

It really hit Joe especially hard, and it was clear he felt guilty about it. "I know we had to be first to Mars, but I rushed it too much. We just weren't ready." Even though Steve and others told him he shouldn't blame himself, he felt like a total failure. Now, regrettably, they had to let all of earth know that the first family on Mars had died and wouldn't be coming back. Earth's inhabitants, however, would not be so forgiving.

The media went crazy with the story that the crew had died on Mars. People were protesting all around the world that lives were unnecessarily put at risk. The greatest protests, though, were right at Mission Control. Protestors were throwing rocks through windows and throwing torches through the broken windows. Others were attempting to loot items from inside Mission Control. Finally, the whole area had to be sealed off. Joe and his staff were out of a job. The Mars mission came to a screeching halt.

Chapter 24

The Price is Right

He was back in Dr. Gonzalez' office, two years later. Where had the time gone since the loss of their first family on Mars? No one even talked about it anymore. The world had moved on to other issues, other stories, other things to protest. Joe entered the waiting room, the same room he had visited so many times over the years. Joe walked into the office and spoke with Trudy, the receptionist. At this moment it occurred to him for some reason that Dr. Gonzalez goes through a lot of receptionists. Maybe it's because they all look to be about 18 years old and then they move on to their next job. Or it could be that the doc just doesn't pay them that well. "I'm here for my 4:00 appointment."

"Go ahead and take a seat in the waiting room."

Joe started flipping channels on the television, going past news shows and soap operas. He was hoping to find a game show and came across The Price is Right.

"Did you know that this is the world's longest running TV game show?" asked Joe.

"Really?" asked Trudy.

"I'm old enough to remember when Bob Barker hosted it."

"Who?"

"Never mind."

"Well, if you know it so well maybe you should go on it and win a fortune."

"I may need to do that, given we lost our funding for the Mars program."

"The doctor will see you now in room two."

"Thanks." Joe walked back to room two where the doctor was ready for him.

"Long time no see Joe. You are usually on time every year for your checkup. Now it's been two years."

"I just had to get away for awhile after we lost our Mars crew. I felt responsible. We should have been able to save them."

"I thought you figured that out. Didn't you find a wormhole above the Martian surface? Did you ever investigate that?"

"Sorry, doc. Nobody believes in wormholes. You remember what happened here 17 years ago. We know what we found, but people just shrugged it off. No one was going to fund an investigation into a wormhole near Mars. After this mission my credibility is blown. Our Mission Control headquarters was trashed and still sits there vacant."

"What about all you learned about Mars because of this trip? That has to be valuable."

"It will take a long time to live this down before anyone will listen to anything about a Mars mission. The only mission they are willing to accept is the one that brings back our astronauts' bodies, if that is even possible. That would involve risking more astronauts, but popular demand may make that happen, although they may lynch me before then. It's not just a matter of hopping on a rocket and bringing them back. Just like this trip took planning, there is a lot of preparation to get humans to Mars and back. Even with all we did for this trip, it just wasn't enough. How unstable will earth's weather have to become before people see the importance of these missions? It wasn't enough when Miami had to be abandoned because it became too expensive to keep it above water. All those people lost their land and were never compensated."

"I'm telling you we still have a good thing here if it were properly managed. Kind of like your health. On that note, after I check all your vitals I want you to go home and fast for 12 hours before you come back so I can do some tests that are overdue. Do you think you can manage that?"

"Whatever you say doc. But we still need Mars as a backup plan."

Chapter 25

Goldilocks

The crew awoke from sleep, unaware of how long they had been out. Captain Dave felt disoriented, unsure of where he was and what was going on. Then he realized, of course, that they were in the spaceship, approaching Mars. But how did he end up in the Captain's chair? He never before went to sleep in the Captain's chair. If he was sitting in the Captain's chair, it was for a reason. If he was in this chair, he was closely monitoring the situation. Then why had he fallen asleep? What was the situation? He turned to his left and saw his wife and first mate Kate, with her eyes closed, sitting at her station. That too seemed odd. "Kate?"

"Just five more minutes," she said.

"No, Kate, remember? We're on the ship. Check the controls in front of you. Are we still on autopilot?"

Kate opened her eyes and got her focus. "Ow! My head! What happened last night?" She realized where they were and checked the control panel. "Autopilot? Yes, we still are, but something is wrong. We're heading *away* from Mars. We're on the edge of the Martian atmosphere. How could we have slept through that? We weren't drinking your secret stash, were we?"

"No, I'd remember that. Whatever happened, the only way to land on Mars now is to switch to manual." Dave took a deep breath, not expecting to be in this situation. "Switching to manual."

About this time their teenage girls had awoken and came to see what all the commotion was about.

"Dad, what are you doing?" asked Kristy. "You don't play video games. You had better let me land it."

"Trust me. I've got this," said Dave as he steered the ship around back in the direction needed to enter the Martian atmosphere. "See, nothing to it." Just then a warning alarm sounded.

"There seems to be some sort of cloud ahead," said Kate. "The computer advises we use caution. Should we send a message to Mission Control?"

"Kate, being this far from earth, Mission Control can only do so much for us. It will take at least 15 minutes for a message to reach them and another 15 minutes after they send us a reply for us to receive it. I doubt they will see anything that we can't."

"Well, it doesn't appear very threatening to me," said their younger daughter Brandy. "It looks like those cumulus clouds we learned about in school. Just a fair-weather thing. You can fly through those like they are not even there."

"My thoughts exactly!" said Dave. "I can't believe we agreed on that. Anyway, let's forge ahead and get to the surface where our comfortable Martian habitats are waiting for us."

"Dear," said Kate, "you know those habitats aren't going to be *that* comfortable." "Well, there's no place like home." Dave took them through the cloud and they barely noticed the turbulence. Dave flicked the switch to separate from the larger portion of the ship. They then continued their descent toward the surface.

"Can you see the landing area?" asked Kate.

"I'm sure we're close," said Dave. "We may have drifted off course a bit, having to switch to manual, so we may have to walk to reach the drop off point where the supplies were delivered for us the last few years."

Regardless of the few bumps along the way, nothing could take away from their excitement at this moment when they were about to be the first people to land on Mars. Dave maneuvered the ship into position and safely landed on the planet.

They got into their spacesuits, eager to step foot on the surface. Dave opened the exit door on the side of the ship and rolled out the steps along the side of the ship leading to the surface. After being weightless in space for seven months, they noticed the pull of gravity on their bodies, although just a third of the weight they would be on earth. It was late in the Martian day, and the temperature was an unseasonably warm 7 degrees below zero Fahrenheit. Fortunately, their spacesuits protected them against such extremes in temperature. They made their way down to the dusty, dry Martian surface. There was no breeze, not to mention very little atmosphere.

"Dave, can you get a reading on where we are in relation to our new home?" asked Kate.

"It looks to be less than a half mile walk to the calculated coordinates, just over that hill. Then we can inflate our home and enter."

"I'll race you there," said Kristy.

"You realize all of this is being documented, so people will be watching these events for a long time," said Kate.

"There goes our privacy," said Kristy. They continued on their way and reached the top of the hill in about 12 minutes. They were a bit confused by what they saw.

"Dad," said Brandy, "didn't you say we would be inflating our new habitat when we got here?"

"I must admit that I did say that. We all saw this site with our habitat on the pictures from earth before we ever left."

"Then I guess we all have the same question," said Kate. "How did it get inflated on its own?"

"Well let's get over there and investigate," said Dave. "It would seem odd that something would trigger it to inflate. Is that even possible?" They made their way down the hill to the site. The cameras were still in place as well as one rover nearby. They found they had a far greater concern than just the inflated habitat. What they saw defied explanation...

Their habitat already being set up in place was one thing. Then there was all the ground disturbance they could see around them. But that wasn't their greatest concern. They turned to look behind them, seeing the lander they had arrived in, and to remind themselves of the direction from which they came. They had to do a double take, because they just looked forward over the hill beyond the area of the habitat, seeing the remains of another lander in the distance, crashed on the surface perhaps a mile beyond their habitat. They could see areas that had been excavated and other areas where various rocks, samples and other material had been sorted and stockpiled. *How was this possible? There was a Mars Mission sent ahead of us? And how was it that they crashed on the surface?* But they also occupied *our* habitats! This sounded too much like Goldilocks and the Three Bears. They walked toward what was supposed to be their habitat. It was all set up in place all right. Dave opened the entrance to the habitat, and they all entered and shut the outside door. Once they were sure they were sealed in from the outside they opened and entered the interior door.

They entered the main central living area. It sure appeared to have been lived in previously. Kate noticed many of the items she personally had selected to decorate the place that were already set up in place. "I couldn't have already done that, right?" she asked. There were family pictures and other personal items all in place. No one else would have done that.

"This is too weird," said Brandy.

"Is it safe to remove our spacesuits in here?" asked Kristy. "I have to scratch an itch somewhere."

Dave checked the readings on the air. "Yes, the air is breathable. We are safely sealed from the outside."

"Great!" said Kristy. "I'm taking this suit off."

"Wait," said Brandy. "Define *breathable*."

"It's fine sweetie," said Kate. "There's enough oxygen remaining to sustain us."

"Comparable to 10,000-foot elevation on earth," said Dave. "Just don't go running around the place. Since our equipment is set up in the habitat, I'm going to send a signal to Mission Control on our classified frequency so they know we landed. They've got some explaining to do."

"So what about that other lander out there?" asked Kate. "I'm sure we can get some answers over there about what happened here."

"I'm coming!" said Kristy.

"Too late," said Brandy. "You took your spacesuit off to scratch yourself. Don't miss a spot."

"Stop it!" said Kristy. "I don't itch anymore, and I'm coming." Kristy quickly began putting her suit on and heading for the door. "I want to find out what's going on."

"I see all the food here has been eaten," said Kate. "That raises even more questions. Another government couldn't have sent a crew that used our supplies, right?"

"If I search the computer, maybe that will tell us something," said Dave.

"Don't look now," said Brandy, "but Kristy is already out the door."

"We might as well all go while we still have our spacesuits on," said Dave. "By the time we return, Mission Control should have received our signal, and then I'll tell them what we found." So they all headed over to the crashed lander to have a closer look and get some answers. It was a bit longer walk than it appeared to be. It was surprising how many small rocks were on the surface, so they had to watch their steps carefully.

"Kristy, be careful," said Kate. "You're getting too far ahead, and I can barely see you."

"I'm fine, mom," she replied back. "It's not like I'm going to catch my hair on anything." Kristy was an excellent runner. That's one way she kept in good physical shape in preparation for the trip, and also made good use of the treadmill on the spaceship. As she got closer to the lander it became obvious to her that it was just like the lander they arrived in, except of course for the fact that it had obviously crashed on the surface hard and sustained major damage. She arrived and stopped right in front of the lander and examined the outside first. It had the familiar markings that were also on their lander. She was curious to see if she could get it open and see inside. She found the hatch, which was severely damaged. The handle and lock were broken, and the hinges were loose. She tugged on it this way and that and to her surprise was able to open it without much difficulty. In fact, the door fell off and dropped to the ground. "Maybe we'll find some spare parts in here if we need them." She climbed inside and maneuvered her way through the mangled insides of the lander, passing through the interior door into the main compartment. Since its hull had been compromised and clearly there was no breathable air in here, she kept her spacesuit on, hoping she didn't have another itch. She switched on her headlamp to find her way in the darkness. "Hello, is anybody home?" For some reason she expected to walk into spider webs, but of course, there were no spiders. She shined her light in various directions, realizing the interior of the lander was just as familiar as the exterior. "This is *our* lander." When she got a good look deeper in the room, she let out a scream.

"Kristy! Is that you?" shouted Kate, after hearing the scream come through on her helmet speaker. They all began running toward the lander, now in a panic, when Brandy tripped on a rock and fell, tearing the right leg of her suit just a couple of inches above her ankle.

"Help! I think I'm leaking air! How can this be happening? These are supposed to be triple puncture resistant." Air was whistling through the tear in her suit. She tried to cover it with her hand. She realized she couldn't stand up and walk while holding the leak at the same time. She knew without something to stop the leak, she would never make it back before running out of air.

"I've got tape!" Dave said, and ran to her, checking the leak.

"Kristy! Can you hear me?" asked Kate.

"I'm okay," said Kristy. "But there are bodies in here."

"What?!" said Kate. "We're coming!"

Dave pulled the tape out of his pocket. "It's a good thing your mom put this in my pocket. I know it's hers because it has pictures of kittens all over it."

"Is it going to be all right?"

"I have enough tape to seal it. That will hold it fine until we get back in the habitat." Her dad helped her up. The tape had stopped the leak, at least for now. They continued on their way together toward the lander. Kate had gotten ahead of them and climbed in through the hatch and located Kristy inside. She had to use her headlamp too.

"Mom, this isn't good," said Kristy. "That's *our* dead bodies lying there. How can that be? We just got here! And we're all fine." There was no doubt about the fact that they were looking at their own bodies there, frozen on Mars.

"You're right about one thing, honey," said Kate. "We're fine. Regardless of what we see, we're alive."

"We must be seeing the future, our future! We're going to die here! Somehow, someway. We can't change that." said Kristy.

Dave and Brandy entered into the lander, hearing the conversation on their head speakers.

Brandy flashed her light on the bodies to add to the light and kept staring at them along with Kristy. "Stop staring at your bodies, girls," said Kate. "That's the kind of thing that will give you nightmares."

"But mom, for once Kristy is right," said Brandy.

"Hey! That sounds like a not compliment." said Kristy.

"Look at me!" said Brandy. "I mean, the dead me. I'm wearing the same spacesuit, with the same tape dad just put on it, discolored and worn."

"That's definitely mom's tape with those baby kittens on it," said Kristy.

"Kristy, *all* kittens are babies," said Brandy. "You don't say baby kittens."

"You do if they're as small and cute as these," said Kristy.

"What happens if I pull my tape off?" said Brandy.

"She's already dead," said Kristy. "Leave her alone."

"Not *her* tape. *My* tape. Will it make her tape disappear because I'm not wearing it?"

"If you take your tape off, it will make the hole bigger, and I won't have enough tape left to keep that sealed tight until our return," said Dave. "Somehow it's safe to conclude that's us in the future if we stay here."

"This is certainly our lander," said Kate.

"Okay, we've seen enough here," said Dave. "There's a spaceship out there and it's leaving now!"

"But what about the mission, and all that we found here?" asked Kate.

"We have no food, and if we leave now we won't be around to die here," said Dave. "End of story."

"I suppose that is true," said Kate. "But obviously something is out of the ordinary here, like how long our bodies have been here, and what the date is now. And what caused that crash."

"Good questions, but let's just get back to *our* lander and set a course for earth," said Dave. "Obviously, we need to get out of here while we still can."

"We had better contact Mission Control first," said Kate. "There must be an explanation for this. What if we just end up crashing again while trying to take off and that's how we die?"

"Kate, let me ask you something," said Dave. "Do you remember eating three months' worth of food? Do you remember *anything* about living three months on Mars?"

"No, I have no memory at all of that."

"And neither do I. So taking off and crashing again doesn't explain where all that food went. We leave now, we change history! We live!"

"Please Dave," said Kate. "At least send a message to Mission Control. It won't hurt anything, and it may help us. Somehow *they* spent three months here and ate all the food before dying here."

"Very well. There's still several hours until daybreak. We'll send a message and come daylight, we're out of here."

Chapter 26

The Response

Joe returned the next day to the office as the doctor had directed. Right away Trudy the receptionist spotted him. "Bob Barker was a vegetarian, even before that was popular, and he lived a good long life."

"I see you have been doing some research," said Joe.

"Yes, but why didn't you tell me?"

"Tell you that he was a vegetarian?"

"No! Tell me that you actually were on The Price is Right."

"What are you talking about?"

"I looked up past contestants and for some reason searched your name. You were on The Price is Right in 1976. You actually met Bob Barker!"

"Do you realize how long ago that was and how old I would have been? Certainly not old enough to be on The Price is Right."

Well, I guess that's true. But how many Joe Schmoes could there be?"

"How many indeed!"

"Well, the doctor will see you now in room two." Joe headed down the hall to room two. He entered and took a seat to wait for the doctor. He looked on the back of the door and noticed that the food pyramid had been replaced by a food octagon with the word STOP written across the middle of it. Then he thought about how *he* had stopped eating for 12 hours so they could draw his blood. Dr. Gonzalez entered the room.

"So I need to confirm that you really did fast so these tests aren't for nothing. I'm trying to avoid unnecessary do overs. When you've been a doctor as long as I have, you learn a few things."

"Yes doc, I *always* follow your instructions," said Joe with a smirk.

"Okay, then roll up your left sleeve." As he was rolling up his sleeve, Joe's phone began buzzing with texts coming through. The doctor looked at Joe as Joe looked at his phone.

"Didn't you see the sign in the waiting room about turning your phone off?"

"Yeah, I saw it. I just never thought you would enforce it. Anyway, I don't get why these messages are coming through from Steve now. He says there's a message from Mars. This message is over two years old." Just then Joe's phone started ringing.

"We really need to discuss the use of your phone in my office."

"Sorry. It's Steve calling. I don't hear much from him anymore. I hope it's not another protest. The last one cost me a fortune. Did I tell you I had to move after they kept coming to my house?" Joe turned away from the doctor and answered his phone. "Hello."

"Dude!" said Steve. "Are you reading my texts? We got a message from Mars, today! Your astronauts are alive!"

"That's impossible! We know they died two years ago."

"Well apparently, they got over it, because I'm receiving a signal on our mission's frequency. They could only be broadcasting that if they got the computer turned on in the habitat. That means they are alive on the surface of Mars."

"Wait Steve," said Joe. "With Mission Control destroyed, how are you getting that signal?"

"I set up an app and put it on my phone. Just a gut feeling that I should track any possible activity. But to check any message, we have to go down to Mission Control and log in."

"Could it just be a malfunction?"

"A malfunction can't send a signal. Somebody is up there. Somebody is alive."

"Two years later? How could they have survived? Okay, I'll be right there. I just have to think through how this is possible and what is our next move." Joe hung up and looked back at the doctor. "Doc, we know they're dead, but they're still alive. What's your diagnosis?"

"Isn't it obvious?"

"Should it be?"

"Joe, all this time you've been looking for wormholes and talking about time travel. Even though their deaths are in *our* past, it is still in *their* future. They haven't made that trip yet that leads to their death."

"That's it! Thanks! No wonder I pay you so much. So one of their trips through the wormhole jumped them to this point in the future, and they are going to go back through the wormhole again, going back in time and dying in the past.

We know it will happen because *it did happen.* I don't think I can rewrite history."

"That doesn't sound like the Joe I know. You can't just give up. You have to figure out how to *keep* them from dying, how to keep them from following that path where they land on Mars again and end up dying there. You have to get them home *now*, while you have the chance."

"You're right doc. I have to go, even if it might blow a hole in the space time continuum."

"Now *that's* the Joe I know."

Shortly later, at Mission Control, or what was left of it

Joe met Steve back at their offices that had been used as Mission Control. They had not been to this complex for well over a year, given that protesters had rendered it useless and they had not made any repairs. "It's a good thing I still have all of my keys," said Joe, "including this key to the front gate." Joe unlocked the gate and opened it up so they could drive to the building. "Hop in with me, Steve, and we'll ride in together. Call me old fashioned, but I still like driving my own car instead of having the car do the driving."

"Well, it is true you hardly ever see that anymore, given all the studies showing how dangerous it is to drive your car manually. I can't believe how people risked their lives driving for so many years."

"Of course, I'm not driving high like most of the people in those studies, or most people on the road."

"True, but it's only a matter of time before the cars won't have a manual mode and the only option will be the car's self-driving mode. Too many people keep switching over to manual so they can act out road rage. There's more road rage now than before autonomous vehicles."

"Then I'll just keep my old 2023 Camry. They last forever anyway. I'm about to hit 250,000 miles." Joe drove in through the gate rather than switch on the self-driving feature. He caught his breath and looked over at Steve. "It's been a long time, Steve."

"Too long. Almost two years since I've seen you."

"So have you found work all this time?"

"I've been getting by going to functions as Captain America. After all, my last name is Rogers. I'm a natural. When kids see my Really Really Real ID 2.0 from DMV, they really believe I'm Captain America. Of course, in January I have to replace it with the Really Really Real ID 3.0, because this one will be worthless after that. Looks like we'll be replacing these every year, just to prove who we are. That, along with our social security numbers now being 18 digits, will keep us all safe. We can certainly be thankful for that, even though my grandfather hasn't been keeping up and now can't prove who he is." They arrived at the main building and got out of Joe's car.

"Steve, I don't know how long technology can stay a step ahead of the hackers. As long as there are people set on causing harm, this digital society will continue to have its drawbacks."

"Joe, weren't you the one who said that one day all the financial records could be in ruins and the money worthless."

"That's another story, but *there's* a reason to move to Mars. No hacking possible on Mars, at least not yet." Joe put his key in the door lock and turned it. He pulled on the door and it opened in a cloud of dust. "Okay, my front door key works and we're in." In the main control room was the equipment that made it possible for them to send communications to Mars, if it would still function. They could also receive any messages that may have been sent. Joe shared with Steve his conversation with the doctor regarding his explanation of how the crew could still be alive while Steve checked the equipment and looked for a message.

"So you're saying they are going to take off, turn back around again toward Mars, and land in the past, where they will spend three months on Mars and then crash when they take off again," said Steve. "We already witnessed that two years ago."

"It's the only explanation for how they can still be alive."

"Well, Joe, I found a message from them in here, so they definitely are alive. Not only are they alive, but they found their own dead bodies and their wrecked lander, the same one they just landed safely in. And all their supplies are used up, so they are taking the next train out of there. That's Dave's words."

"So there's *two* landers? And *two* of each astronaut, one alive and one dead? Okay, that makes perfect sense."

"What are you talking about, Joe? That makes no sense!"

"It's just the way they left it two years ago. They are crossing paths with their future selves. In their timeline they haven't made that trip yet, so when they take off they'll land two years in the past before all that happened and use their supplies and crash. They just don't know it yet. But perhaps, just *perhaps*, this is our chance to *change* what happened. We can intervene in *their* future."

"But how do we get them to do something different than what they already did? It's not like we can just send them a message to do something different. What they did is a result of what they are experiencing now, along with whatever we tell them. We already know the outcome."

"Steve, *we* have to do something different than what we would normally do to get *them* to do something different. Since it hasn't happened to *them* yet, they can still make a different choice. We have to outthink the timeline we already experienced."

"Well Joe, knowing you, you would have gotten our staff together to analyze the situation and made sure you got the information we were going to send to them *just right* to ensure they get out safely and don't land again."

"Yeah, right! What staff?" Joe looked around in all directions as if to check for staff. "But you're right. I would have found them and we would have worked out the best solution. We would have made sure it was politically correct and could not lead to lawsuits. I would have conferred with my attorney who would have searched online for the answer and charged me for every minute of it. I would have complained about what he was charging me, leading to more delays. Wait! That's it! You know Dave. He's not that patient and if he feels he just has to make a decision and he thinks he has it figured out, he won't wait for a message. He'll decide to take off on his own while we're still planning the perfect response."

"You do like giving the perfect response, Joe, but you're right. There's no time for that. You just have to give *any* response, and maybe *the wrong* response, if you have to, before *he* makes the wrong decision. You need to send it *now.* You can't let him get on that next train. Make a quick voice recording and send it. There's no time for typing it out and editing it, like you're some famous author."

"You're right Steve, but what if the wrong decision I send him is what gets them killed?"

"No, that's what you would have thought. You have to forget that possibility."

"Yes, we've wasted too much time already. It will still take another 15 minutes to reach them. So here it goes." Joe turned on the transmitter, spoke his message while Steve sat there listening, and sent it. "Okay, hopefully they'll get that in about 15 minutes. By the way Steve, when did Dave send that last message? Are we already too late?"

"Well it was several hours since that first signal started. Let me see when we actually received this message. Looks like about five hours ago. When was the next train coming?"

"He probably meant at first light of day on Mars. I have no idea now when that would be. We may already be too late. That could be what kills them. I knew we couldn't change the past. That's crazy, right? We're doing the only thing we would have done, just going through the motions leading to what we know already happened. It's not like *we* have done this before."

"Don't give up hope Joe. You never know. It's still *their* future, and it's not set in stone. They can still make whatever choices they want. All we can do now is wait and see what happens."

Chapter 27

Crossroads

Back on Mars, Martian time was moving fast and running out. Dave checked the time, and it was just as he suspected. "It's been five hours since we sent that message and there's no response from Mission Control," said Dave. "If we really are in another year, they may not even have received our message. The sun is rising. It's time to get on the ship and leave for home. If they got the message, I'm sure we'll hear from them on the way home."

"But they must have *some* explanation for what happened," said Kate.

"Which we'll find out on the way home!" said Dave.

"Okay, I suppose that makes sense," said Kate. "I've just got a bad feeling about this, like we made the wrong choice once and are about to do it again."

"If that were true Mission Control would realize it as well and alert us, but we've got nothing. Staying here won't save us. We know what we have to do."

"Very well."

"But what about our bodies?" asked Brandy. "We can't just leave them here."

"Yeah," said Kristy. "I want to take my dead body back and show it off at school. No one else in school has their own dead body. Of course, I'll have to mummify it first. How do you do that anyway? I'll find a YouTube video. Oh, wait! No WiFi."

"No one is taking their bodies," said Dave. "We can't have decomposing bodies on a spaceship, and why are we even discussing this?"

"Okay, but I'm still taking pictures," said Kristy. "I want proof."

"That's so morbid!" said Brandy.

"Yeah, my friends will love it," said Kristy. "Wait! Dad, if we really are in the future, did you ask them if they have flying cars? There must be flying cars if it's the future."

"Kristy, flying cars are at least thirty years in the future," said Dave, "if not further. I don't think we went that far. Just be happy with your autonomous car. When I was growing up I had to drive mine manually."

"I know dad. You told us a hundred times. And wait, I remember, it ran on regular unleaded. I don't even know what that means. Sometimes I think you just make this stuff up."

"It's time to say goodbye to Mars," said Dave. "If there's anything you want to take from this habitat, grab it now. Our train is ready for departure."

"For some reason I'm feeling deja vu, like we've done this before," said Kate.

"Must be all that practice in the simulator," said Dave. Just then a message came in on the computer.

"We got a response!" said Kate. "What does it say?" Dave played the message, cranking it up for all to hear:

This is Joe. Please listen carefully. How do I say this? You have been caught in a time loop of sorts, a wormhole hovering just above your landing site. The whole world believes you died on Mars two years ago, after spending three months there and crashing on takeoff, which explains your bodies being there. We have your entire trip documented. It's just that, you've been going through that wormhole several times and landing on Mars in different years, either the past or the future. We believe you make that final trip, going back in time two years and spending three months on Mars, after you take off now. Each time you pass through the wormhole you forget that you previously passed through it. Apparently, the time displacement or something else about the wormhole affects short term memory. We're not sure what exactly causes it. What you are planning to do now is to take off and head for home, since your supplies have been exhausted. The problem is, once you take off and pass through the wormhole, you will forget that you were ever on the surface, just as you did before, so you will turn around and land again, and think you have just arrived. It is then that you radio to us that you have arrived safely but for some reason are low on fuel. When we got that message, we understood that the reason is, you have been using your fuel landing and taking off without recalling that. Your lander will also get damaged, and you will be unable to attach it to the ship after that. That's what will cause you to crash and die.

Since you are now getting this message while you are still alive, and before making that trip that causes the damage to your lander, there may still be a way to prevent you from dying then. The only way to prevent that is to take off and return to earth now. I know that is your plan, but you need to find a way to tell yourselves to do that even though you won't remember you ever landed. You need to convince yourselves once your memory is erased to go back to earth rather than turn the ship around and land on Mars again. What you do now before you leave your shelter and take off in the lander will determine if you make it home. Do the right thing. We'll be cheering for you.

"Okay," said Dave. "It looks like we're going home then."

"Before we go anywhere, what are we going to do to *make sure* we know what to do, even if we lose our memory?" asked Kate. There was a pause while they all reflected on what to do.

"I've got an idea," said Kristy.

"So do I," said Brandy.

"Are you sure your ideas will help us remember what to do?" asked Kate. Both girls confidently assured their mom of that and said they would share their ideas on the way to the ship. They all went searching through their habitat for anything they would like to bring with them and anything that might help them remember what they needed to do. Then they took the walk across the landscape back toward the lander, confident that they were prepared. As they were walking, Kate noticed what looked like some scrap metal on the surface of Mars. "This looks like it came off one of our satellites, in fact, there's Joe Schmoe's logo right on it."

"It looks like it was used for something," said Dave. "We removed big chunks of this. Maybe we used it in our future, two years ago, when we come back."

"But we're not coming back," said Kristy. "So if we're not coming back, we're *not* using this, right? And yet, it *was* used. Just like, our bodies are *still* out there. Shouldn't they disappear, because we're making the right choice?"

"It's very timey wimey," said Brandy. "We're changing the past, so we don't come back and die. We don't plan to be around to see history correct itself here, but it will. As long as we don't return, our dead bodies will vanish, I think." They continued on their way and arrived at the lander.

"It's like we were just here yesterday," said Kristy. "I know that we were, but I just wish we could have stayed longer. That three-month visit didn't happen to us yet, and if we aren't returning, we'll have no memory of it."

"Right now the important thing is to get home safe," said Dave. "Something tells me that won't be as easy as we think. Everything we've seen on this planet tells us we *did*, or we *do* come back and die here. We have to prevent that from happening."

"It'll work," said Kristy. "We'll remember what to do."

"For some reason I think that's only part of the challenge," said Dave. "If we lost our memories, what actually happened to us to cause that to occur?" Dave turned and looked behind them, then turned back ahead to board the lander. He realized that their questions would be answered soon enough. They all made their way up the stairs. Dave looked back over the horizon just before entering the lander. "Did I say everything I *needed* to say, for history's sake?"

"You did fine dad," said Kristy. "We're proud of you."

"I'm getting you all back safe," said Dave. "I promise." He stepped aboard the lander and his family followed. Then they all got in their positions, ready for blastoff.

"Okay, Dave, take us home," said Kate, "after one last kiss before I strap myself in. And this is not goodbye."

"You got it," said Dave. "When we get back, I'm taking you on a date you'll never forget."

"That's what I thought *this* was," said Kate. Of course, then she realized that she had forgotten quite a bit.

"Everybody, remember who you are and where we're going," said Dave as he fired up the rocket. He gave an audible countdown from ten down to one, shouted "Liftoff!" and they lifted off the surface, rising further above Mars. All the while Kristy was repeating her name under her breath. He plotted a course for the main ship in orbit.

"It's going to be a long trip home," said Brandy.

"Well, we still have board games on the ship. Wait, you distracted me. I'm trying to remember my name. Kristy, Kristy, Kristy. As long as I keep repeating it, we'll be fine."

"Don't worry," said Brandy. "You won't forget your name." Their lander approached the main part of the ship in orbit and successfully docked with it and they continued on their way in one piece.

"See, nothing to it," said Dave. "We're doing fine." *They'll be calling me Admiral soon.* Dave watched their elevation continue to climb until he saw it ahead of him. They approached what they now understood was a wormhole. There was no way to avoid it. It was as if it was waiting for them.

"We're just going into this harmless cumulus cloud on our way home," said Kristy. "It can do that on autopilot."

"I'm holding on to the controls, just in case," said Dave. "We don't know what that thing is capable of, but right now it's our only way out of here. We get through this and we're home free. Here we go. Everyone stick to the plan." Kate noticed that their readings approaching the wormhole were different than when they passed through approaching Mars. Was that because they were working against gravity now, putting more strain on the system? Or was there just something different about this side of it? Or had it changed composition since they last approached it? She had more questions than she realized, with no clear answers, as they began their entry into the cloud.

"By the way, I forgot to ask," said Brandy, "but who wrote VGER on the side of the ship?"

"Never mind that," said Kate. Then she looked up and gasped in shock. "What in the world is *that*?" They saw what looked like a giant funnel pulling in all sorts of debris, getting tighter and tighter as far as they could see until it appeared to disappear altogether in the distance. They could feel it pulling them in and there was nothing they could do about it. They were rapidly increasing in speed and the ship began to vibrate. "I'm sure that wasn't there a minute ago. There was no sign of this before we entered the cloud."

"That's got to be a black hole," said Brandy. "No one has ever gone through one of those."

"Don't be silly, Brandy," said Kate. "It can't be a black hole. There wouldn't be a black hole right in our solar system. We've got space maps a million light years in every direction with no evidence of a black hole. With all the study of Mars and its vicinity, this would have been observed and documented. So there's no way a black hole could form here. It's just something else, something we can't explain. Explain it, Dave!"

Dave was starting to wonder if this was like the Bermuda Triangle of space that would become a spaceship graveyard with no escape. "My navigation charts are just spinning," said Dave. "There's no way to track our location. It's like we're nowhere and everywhere all at the same time. We may not even be anywhere near Mars anymore. There's no way to turn back. And I know this question doesn't make much sense, but does anyone remember what day this is?"

"It's Friday!" said Kate. "Wait! Why did I say that? How old am I? I can't remember. This thing is messing with our concept of time. Let's not forget what day it is."

"It's no day," said Kristy. "It doesn't matter what day it is. Every day is the same, yesterday, today and tomorrow." Kristy began to dance around the spaceship without a care in the world, seeming to be unaware of where they were or that they were in any danger. "Come on, Brandy. Dance with me!"

"Stop it!" said Brandy. "Something is going on in your head. You're acting goofier than normal. You need to secure yourself in a seat. Why don't you just go back to repeating your name over and over again?" Dave had no control over the ship and it just went where the funnel took them. It seemed as if all matter within the ship was being compressed and deformed due to this gravitational field. He was concerned that the ship would be torn apart, but it held together. Then, in an instant, they found themselves in unfamiliar territory in open space, just drifting. "Okay, we're free, so where are we?" asked Dave. "Bring up the space charts and get a pin on our location."

"Wherever it is, it looks like somewhere that we don't want to be," said Kate. They found themselves on the scene of a massive explosion deep in space. Debris was flying in every direction, much of it on fire. Radiation readings were off the charts. It's as if they just missed the war but were feeling the consequences.

"Dad, where are we?" asked Brandy.

"We just entered that cloud. We couldn't have been traveling for more than a minute. But Mars is gone!" said Dave.

"You mean it exploded?" asked Brandy.

"That can't be right," said Kate. "Actually, there must be something wrong with our instruments. Based on these readings, we're over 40 million miles away from where we just were, and no closer to earth. We're also under attack."

"Aliens?" asked Kristy. "I think we were promised there would be aliens, and then cake if we won. I'm hoping for white cake with cream cheese frosting."

"No. It's a storm of rocks," said Dave. "It's like we just got here after something exploded. But what would cause such an explosion? I'm trying to avoid taking on damage or we won't be going anywhere. Hopefully the ship's sensors can protect us from the debris, like they were designed to do." Waves of radiation were bombarding the ship, even if they managed to evade the debris.

"At least the sensors were built in Japan," said Kristy. "All the good stuff comes from Japan, where they work 20-hour days after people figured out how to live without sleep. I want to learn how to live without sleep so I can get more done."

"How could we have traveled 40 million miles almost instantaneously?" asked Kate, "and if that's true, can we get home?" It appeared that the long trip home was getting longer.

"I told them to put a laser gun on this ship so we could blast stuff like that," said Kristy. "Why weren't we given a laser gun? All the big crime organizations on earth have laser guns. Why couldn't we get one stinking laser gun? I'm sure we could have negotiated for one in the Tex Mex neutral zone. And did you know Tex Mex used to be a kind of food before it became a neutral zone? I read that somewhere. Am I rambling? I think black holes make me ramble."

"Ok. I'm done talking to Kristy. I think if we veer off to our left we can escape the effect of whatever that was," said Brandy. "It will also get us out of danger of being struck by debris."

Dave could still see the funnel, and possibly their route back to Mars, behind them. "No, if I lose this funnel, we are lost in space, too far from earth with no hope of getting home. Our only hope is to go back the way we came, if that's possible." It was also unclear how long that funnel had been there or how long it would remain intact. Their instruments weren't much help in answering that.

"Dave," said Kate, "I see something at two o'clock. It looks like another ship."

"It's not just *another* ship," said Dave. "It's *our* ship. It's a ship that looks exactly like ours."

"There's another ship at ten o'clock," said Kristy.

"And look!" said Brandy, "another ship straight ahead."

"This must be where we came each time we came through the cloud," said Dave, "and *when* we came in. No matter what date it was each time we left Mars, we end up here at a single point in time when this explosion took place."

"So what are our options?" asked Kate.

"There's really only one viable option," said Dave. "We go back the way we came. It's our only chance of getting home." Clearly, it was more than just a funnel. Just as matter could travel through in this direction, there was a path alongside that funnel pulling matter in the opposite direction. If they followed that path, supposedly it would take them back where they were, hopefully back near Mars, from which they could still head home to earth.

"If all those ships are ours, is that the choice we always made?" asked Kristy.

"Why would we make a different choice? That's suicide," said Dave.

"Why don't we wait to see if one of the other ships goes the other way?" asked Brandy. "Let's find out what happens to them before we decide."

"What if that's what the other ships are waiting to see?" asked Kate. "They're thinking like us, because they *are* us."

"That means that if we go the other way, they may follow," said Dave. "But we know *they* made it back to Mars, so they must have gone back the way they came. Mission Control only built us one ship, so that's just us arriving from different points in time. We all somehow came to *this* point in time and space where this explosion was occurring."

"So if we decide *not* to go back the way we came," said Kate, "they may follow and no one gets back to Mars, and we change the past, but not necessarily for the best."

"Look!" said Kristy. "The ship at two o'clock is turning and going back into that funnel."

"That's our next move too," said Dave. "We know where that takes us. They make it back and we'll make it back."

"What if we wait to see if they all go?" asked Brandy. "What if going back just sends us into an endless loop?"

"They're thinking the same thing," said Dave. "The longer we wait, the more likely someone will make the wrong choice, which could end it for all of us. If any of those ships makes a different decision than the one they made that got us this far, it may break the timeline and with it, us."

"Do we really know that?" said Kate. "We have been stuck in a trap this whole time. This may be our way out. At least then we won't lose our memories."

"We're too far from home here. If we keep arguing over this back and forth," said Dave, "the choice will be made for us. I'd rather make that choice myself."

"A second ship is going back," said Kristy.

"The others are still holding their positions," said Kate. "Is there a way to communicate with another ship? We're all using the same frequency."

"That's not possible," said Dave. "I can't imagine talking with ourselves."

"It can't hurt anything," said Kate. "I'm going to try hailing them." Just then Dave noticed a new flashing light on his control panel.

"Wait!" said Dave. "*We're* being hailed. Apparently, we decided to attempt communication. I'll open the channel on our computer."

They heard the voice coming through on the open channel. *Do you read us? Come in. Come in.*

"Yes," said Dave. "We hear you loud and clear."

We were leaving Mars on our way back to earth and ended up here.

"So were we. What happened when you were on Mars?"

We were supposed to spend three months there, but for some reason our supplies never arrived, so we had to leave. We went through something like a black hole and ended up here.

"Really?" said Dave. "Hold please while I consult my team." Dave placed them on mute.

"Dad," said Brandy. "That's *us* from the past. They must have landed in the past before Mission Control sent any supplies. We know they went back and survived, and that has to happen for us to get here."

"That means that we, or *they*, haven't been able to reach Mission Control," said Kristy. "They don't know anything about us landing multiple times. They probably don't recognize that we *are* them. We're just another ship. They're trying to figure out how we can even be here."

"So what happens if they *don't* go back?" asked Kate.

"We all disappear and they will be the only ones left," said Dave, "The timeline that got us here gets cut and they will be stuck out here alone. We have to tell them to go back through the wormhole. Then, we have to follow."

"Okay, agreed," said Kate. Dave took the controls off mute.

"Hello, people leaving Mars," said Dave. "You must return back the way you came."

We barely survived coming through that thing. We thought there might be another way home. Are you sure that is a good idea?

"I guarantee if you go now, you will make it," said Dave. "It's not safe here."

Who are you? We don't know anything about any other ships.

Dave paused for a minute, wondering how he could make them understand. "Dave, I know who you are. Listen to me. I'm from the future. If you want to save Kate, Brandy and Kristy and ever get home, you have to go now. If you don't, *we all die.* There's no time to think about it. It's the right thing to do, please." Dave closed the channel and leaned back in his chair, in a sweat in the cold darkness of space. Kate watched to see what would happen. The seconds felt like hours, earth hours.

"Dave, they're turning back," said Kate. "You did it."

"Okay, that's it," said Dave. "We're turning around."

"If we're doing this," said Kate, "girls, go to your beds and strap yourselves in. This is going to be a very bumpy ride."

"You don't have to tell me twice," said Brandy as they headed for their beds.

"And let's strap ourselves into our chairs as well," said Dave. "I love you all."

"No time for goodbyes Dave," said Kate. "Just take us home." Dave turned the ship around, grateful that he still had navigational control, and headed straight for the wormhole. As he began to feel its effects, he again could no longer control the ship as they were pulled in. Once they entered the funnel, the ship shook violently as if it was going to be torn apart. It was worse than any turbulence they had ever felt. It began to feel like an endless spin. Multiple alarms were sounding that they had no response for. "Hull integrity holding," said Dave. "It won't take much more of this. Just sit tight." The dizziness was unbearable, until they all passed out, leaving the ship subject to the forces of the wormhole without their help. The ship finally cleared the cloud and stabilized back over Mars, continuing on its forward momentum traveling away from Mars. It would appear that they had made it through in one piece.

Chapter 28

Revelation

As Brandy opened her eyes, at first all she heard was silence. She tried to gather her thoughts and recall what she was doing before she fell asleep. Well, she was in space. She was on a mission to Mars. She had spent several months, at least seven months, in space. She hadn't seen a cute boy or had a decent meal in months. She had been weightless for months. She must have gone to sleep in her bed on the spaceship. After all, that's where she always slept. But something wasn't right. Her surroundings had changed. She was no longer in her bed. She wasn't on the spaceship. She wasn't on Mars. The air was breathable. She was no longer weightless but felt the full weight of gravity, putting more pressure on her body than she was really prepared for. She didn't remember landing anywhere, so how could this be? She was lying on a cold, thinly carpeted floor. She looked up at the ceiling. The only light in the room was natural light from outside that came through the blinds on the windows. It was full sunlight, like she hadn't seen since… She slowly raised her head to look around. She was in a large room with round tables and three or four chairs around each table. The ceiling lights turned on when they sensed the motion, causing her to squint. It looked like an office break room, but a room unfamiliar to her. She slowly stood up on her feet, trying to remember how she got here, but nothing in her head added up to explain her surroundings. She wanted to call out to her family, but not knowing where she was, she realized the need for caution, unaware of whom she might alert to her presence.

She felt sore all over and really just wanted to go back to sleep, but she realized that was probably a bad idea. She heard sounds in the distance coming from an adjoining room and crept in that direction to find out what was going on. As she crept closer she recognized a familiar voice, although not a member of her family. It was Joe. How could *he* be here? Was he responsible for where she found herself? Maybe it was just a recording from Joe that was sent to the family. Surely her family must be nearby. What had happened to their mission? She went through an open doorway into the adjoining room and saw the back of Joe's head, his hair looking whiter than she remembered. He was talking to Steve while focused on the monitor of his computer in front of him on a desk. She continued toward him, coming up from behind. "What was that flash?" Joe asked. "We did *something*. Did it work?"

They had earlier placed a package of supplies in the corner of the room. "Joe, our package vanished, just as we had hoped. If that worked, then what about…" Steve was facing Joe but looked up behind him to see Brandy, who had approached and was about ten feet behind Joe. He gestured to Joe to look behind him. Joe turned around, and as he realized it was Brandy his face lit up. "It worked! You're alive! You made it!" he said.

"What do you mean?" asked Brandy. "Where am I? Where's my family?"

"You're back on earth of course," said Joe. "I got you out of there. The wormhole brought you home. What do you remember last?"

"I'm not sure. I think we were about to land, or were we leaving? Did we make it to Mars? I must have fallen asleep. I woke up here, and I could sure use a couple of Advil. How could I have gotten that close to Mars and ended up back here?"

"Your memories will eventually return. It was how the wormhole affected you. You traveled tens of millions of miles in a matter of seconds. That's extraordinary. I was able to shift the path of the wormhole to bring you back to earth."

"I know, but… Wait a minute! Seconds? How? Never mind. What about my family?" Brandy protested. "If you *got me out of there*, what happened to *them*? Why would you bring me here? What about the mission?"

"We'll find out soon enough about your family. They must be okay this time. We just have to go find them."

"What do you mean, *this time*? What are you talking about? I was just with them a couple of minutes ago! I don't remember any other times."

"Joe, you have to tell her the whole truth," said Steve. "You owe her that much, after all she's been through."

Joe looked from Steve back into Brandy's desperate eyes, that were longing for answers to this mystery. "Yes, of course I'm going to tell her the whole truth. She has to know the whole truth. So here we go, the whole truth. I don't know how to say this," he said, pausing briefly and wiping a tear, or probably several. Brandy never saw Joe appear so nervous, shuffling his hands and clearly shaking while he gathered a complete sentence, and then he said it. "I'm so sorry, Brandy." Joe paused once again to regain his composure. "I'm the one responsible for the wormhole."

"What?" said Brandy. "You know how to make a wormhole, one that could have gotten us all killed?"

"I was looking for a faster way to Mars. We needed a way to send supplies and people without the long journey in space. I experienced the power of a wormhole before when it sent me halfway around the world and back in time. I already had a device that could keep a wormhole open. I couldn't create a wormhole, so I began to search for another wormhole. I had satellites searching the heavens for wormholes, but with little success. I realized they just weren't going to be that easy to find, and there would probably be none anywhere in our solar system. Then I thought about the one in San Francisco that formed as a result of a nuclear explosion. I thought that if it happened once, could it happen again? Well, I couldn't exactly go around setting off nuclear explosions on earth to test my theory, but could I set one off in space to create a wormhole that could be used as a portal between Earth and Mars? It was a long shot, but it was the only shot I had. I had to find a reason to set off a nuclear bomb in space, a reason that no one would suspect what my real motive was, so I located an asteroid and got approval to test if a nuclear bomb could disrupt its course. I really didn't care what happened to the asteroid. I just had to see if I could trigger a wormhole. This one asteroid we located was near the asteroid belt, beyond Mars, but close enough to earth to be within reach. The explosion *did* create a wormhole, and in fact, away from the confines of earth's atmosphere and gravitational pull, it expanded much larger than I thought possible. Although the asteroid was far from Mars, the wormhole that was created had to lead somewhere, and it came out above Mars. It even carried much of the remains of the asteroid to Mars where it showered down on the surface, where you would have seen it if you had returned to Mars in the past. But then, my work became more urgent when the mission failed."

"What do you mean, it failed? They *are* on their way home, right?"

Joe looked back at Steve. Steve nodded to Joe. Joe turned back toward Brandy and took a deep breath to regain his composure. "*You* just saw your family, Brandy, but that was *five years ago*. Because you landed on Mars five times, you used up vital fuel supplies. Your ship was too large for the wormhole to carry it through to the origin point of the explosion, but it did shift you to different points in time each time you landed on the surface of Mars."

"Wait, wait, wait!" said Brandy. "Stop right there! Explosion? I remember. I was there. We saw debris flying everywhere and other copies of our ship. Dad said we traveled 40 million miles."

"So it did take you through and you were able to come back! Anyway, we had hoped that once you left Mars and headed for home you could still make it back to earth by conserving fuel, moving slower and rationing your remaining food. We just hoped that *somehow*, there would be a way, even though the path back to earth was over fifty percent longer than originally planned due to where it was in its orbit at that time, and you had only half the fuel. There was just no way to make that work. The numbers don't lie. You never made it. You all died in space over four years ago. The ship was never recovered."

"But I'm not dead. If you rescued me, you can rescue them. Bring them through the wormhole! Or send me back to spend my last days with my family."

"It's too late for that. We only had one shot to reach back in time at that exact moment five years ago from this exact moment today to pull you out, after precise calculations and planning for it, and it worked. The ship would have kept moving and in a flash be out of the wormhole. The wormhole has since collapsed."

"So how are they okay? You said they died in space!"

"Yes, of course. Four years ago. And it would have stayed that way if we hadn't rescued you. You have to realize that history has been changing a lot since you first left earth eight years ago."

"It doesn't feel like eight years ago to me!" said Brandy. "It's been less than a year for me. I'm still 15 years old, right?"

"Physically you are, but you were born about 22 years ago."

"Great, so you're telling me I can order a drink in a restaurant. I'm still confused, but I will take that drink."

"Let me explain. According to our history you crashed and died on Mars seven years ago, after spending three months there and providing an abundance of data to keep us busy for years. Then you turned up alive five years ago, because you hadn't gone back in time yet to make that final trip where you would have died. Then we were able to keep you from landing again, so you avoided going back in time and crashing in the past. But then when you finally left Mars for good and headed home to earth you all died in space four years ago when your food ran out. I spent the last four years working out how to access you through the wormhole back in time to bring you forward to this moment in time in the hopes of changing that past and saving you all. Now that we were able to access you back five years ago through the wormhole and get you off the ship, we just changed that timeline from that point five years ago. Instead of dying with them on the ship, you are now here alive and well. As part of the plan, though, we had an additional supply of food here. We transported it to the ship at the moment of that flash, the moment you arrived from the ship. Call it an exchange. Hopefully, it made it to the ship, and with one less mouth to feed as well, they should have been able to stretch out their fuel and still have enough food to make it back to earth a little less than four years ago. When I made that exchange a few minutes ago my time, it changed the timeline from that point five years ago and rewrote history. All I remember right now is what I lived before I rescued you. I'm hoping my memories will catch up with the new timeline, since I would have been part of that too, according to my fuzzy math. Anyway, your family may be alive on earth right now. We just have to go look for them."

"In fact," said Steve, "something tells me that if they *did* make it back to earth, they would know by now where to look for you."

"So they should be here!" said Brandy. "Wherever here is, they would know where you were going to bring me back. But they're *not* here. They should be here waiting for me. Something happened. Something went wrong."

Chapter 29

Return

Back on the spaceship, five years earlier, what exactly happened?

Dave awoke from sleep, unaware of what had occurred. He was seated in the Captain's chair, where he had sworn an oath never to fall asleep on the job. At least that oath was just in his head. He turned to his left to see Kate resting in her chair, looking so peaceful. He couldn't recall announcing that they would all take a nap, yet here they were on a peaceful ride through space. Finally, he inquired of his wife, "Are we still on autopilot?"

Kate opened her eyes to find her head spinning, at least on the inside. It actually felt bigger on the inside, like the stuff science fiction is made of. She couldn't really concentrate on anything at first, but slowly she got her bearings. She looked up and checked the control panel and all of its blinking lights. "Yes, but something is wrong. We're heading *away* from Mars. We're on the edge of the Martian atmosphere. How could we have slept through that?"

"Whatever happened, the only way to land on Mars now is to switch to manual."

Dave took a deep breath, not expecting to be in this situation. "Switching to manual." He reached for the switch to go to manual.

"Wait a minute, Dave!" said Kate. "There's a note here that reads: Do not switch to manual again, you idiot! Do not land! Return to earth!"

"What? Who wrote that? That wasn't there before we went to sleep as we were approaching Mars. Probably one of Kristy's practical jokes. I'm switching to manual to land this thing. We can't hang around here wasting fuel." Dave again reached for the switch.

"Wait!" said Kate. "Look up!"

Dave raised his head to see a row of rocks lined up on the shelf just above his head. "Where did all those rocks come from? We didn't bring rocks from earth. Those were definitely not there before."

"They look like something we would have collected on Mars." Kate ran her scanner over one of the rocks, confirming with 95% certainty that it was of Martian origin. "I know we haven't landed yet, but I just dreamed that we collected Mars rocks, and there they are."

"Are you trying to tell me that your dreams are becoming reality? If that's true, I want in."

"Dave, I'm just trying to figure this out." At this point Kristy had woken up and came to see what was going on.

"Your father is trying to figure out why we are heading *away* from Mars and what this note and these rocks are all about," said Kate.

"When I woke up, I found a note too," said Kristy. "It reads: You won't remember this, but you were already on Mars. Check the video camera if you don't believe me, you losers."

Kristy paused for a minute. "That's funny. It sounds like something I would write."

"And there's more on the back," said Kristy. "It reads: You are low on fuel because of already landing on Mars four times. If you land again, you will die there. I wanted to bring my body home and show it off at school but dad wouldn't let me. Return home now and change the past. Yes, it's complicated."

"Honey, for some reason this feels like deja vu all over again," said Kate.

"You can't say, 'deja vu all over again,'" said Kristy. "That's double talk. It's like saying 'baby kittens'".

Dave pulled out the video camera. "I'm checking the video footage now." Dave noticed there was quite a bit of recorded video and looked to see what it included. "From this, someone is telling the truth and apparently we had landed on Mars," said Dave. "There's footage of us leaving the lander and walking on the surface. I don't remember tripping on my way down like that." Dave looked over at his fuel gauge. "Not only that, but our fuel supplies are quite a bit lower than was calculated for. We had to be doing more traveling than we remember. It's like a big block of our memory has been erased. How could that have happened? I'm contacting Mission Control and recommending that we return to earth. The series about our life on Mars will have to be postponed."

"After coming this far I can't believe we're turning back," said Kristy. "I had a lot of commercial shots planned while we were on

Mars. Now I'll just have to double my efforts on the way back home. Maybe I can still get paid for the commercials I don't remember doing. I really wonder what would have made us land and take off all those times."

"Perhaps Mission Control can figure that out when we get back," said Kate.

"We're going to need a better plan from Mission Control," said Dave. "Given the amount of fuel we have, if we conserve by reducing speed, our food supplies will run out. If we continue on at normal speed, there's no way our fuel will get us home."

"Why hasn't Brandy gotten up?" asked Kate. "We had better check on her."

They went to Brandy's bed and she wasn't there. What they did find in her place was a large box marked "Care Package" with a card attached. "How can she be gone? There's no place to go," said Kate. "And where did this come from?" Kate opened the card and read it. "Please find inside enough food and supplies to get you home before you run out of fuel. If this worked as planned, one of you is missing and is (or will be) safely back on earth five years in the future. This was the only way to get all of you home safely. It is also expected that the memory loss you have experienced is only temporary and you should eventually recall your entire time on Mars, or at least the parts that already happened in your timeline. -Joe."

"Brandy is already on earth?" asked Kristy.

"But this says five years in the future," said Kate. "So she is neither here nor there now?"

"Well the answers are waiting for us back on earth, where we will be reunited," said Dave. "I promised I would get us all home safe. Now I am keeping that promise. The ship is set on a course for earth. The Admiral has spoken."

Kate turned to look Dave in the eye. "Honey, I think you mean Captain."

There was no turning back now. The Whitneys made the return trip to earth, just as Joe had planned.

Back at Mission Control after Brandy's return

Joe, Steve, and Brandy walked out of the room where they were reunited and decided to take a look around. Joe popped his head into the main Control room to see it beautifully restored and functional, like it had never been trashed at all. "Steve! Everything changed! People don't hate us anymore, and they didn't destroy Mission Control. The mission must have been successful after all."

"Yes, I remember that now," said Steve. "There was a big celebration when the family returned."

"And when we explained how we were getting you back later through the wormhole," said Joe, "they accepted our explanation and looked forward to your return, trusting us, because generally speaking, people are really good."

"Really?" said Brandy. "Because I thought most people were jerks. Oh! Different timeline! This will take some getting used to."

"Well let's start with your family, because I just got a text," said Steve. "They are outside waiting for us right now."

"Of course!" said Joe. "In the new timeline I would have told them to meet us outside at this exact moment to not interfere with anything that happened before."

"That makes perfect sense!" said Brandy. "Now, don't make another wormhole or I'll stuff you into it."

"Trust me," said Joe. "I've learned my lesson. No more messing with the real timeline that we are now living in. Let's go get you reunited with your family. You still have many missions ahead of you."

Of course, who's to say the "real" timeline couldn't change or be written over again? All it would take is...

About the Author

James Hart threw his personal twist on time travel and the origin of aliens in his Rules of Time trilogy. Now he throws his hat into the space travel experience in Martian Time. His style of writing and humor reflects many of the values he was raised with. Those who know him may find hidden gems in these stories meant for them, whether to make them smile or inspire them to continue on in a challenging world. He hopes his stories will enrich each reader and perhaps inspire them to get out of their comfort zone while discovering what they are capable of, or if that's too much to handle, at least brighten their day.

Other Books by James Hart

The Rules of Time
The Limits of Time
The End of Time